"You can't go yet!"

She moved to block the door bodily with her attractive form.

He smiled down at her. "Sure I can, if only you'll let me by, ma'am. Look, it ain't that I don't admire your company, but I got to meet the Cheyenne night train."

"But it won't be dark for hours. Surely you can stay just a little while? Och, Custis, I've been so *lonely!*"

His voice was gentle as he answered. "I can see that, ma'am. I know the feeling and it hurts. I'd stay an hour or more if I thought it would really help, but it wouldn't, Miss Sine. You'd only wind up alone here in any case."

She looked away, licked her pink rosebud lips, and murmured, "At least stay long enough to love me. I'm sure I'd be able to sleep tonight if only you'd make love to me now...."

TABOR EVANS

LONGARM

AND THE CUSTER COUNTY WAR

A JOVE BOOK

LONGARM AND THE CUSTER COUNTY WAR

A Jove Book/published by arrangement with
the author

PRINTING HISTORY
Jove edition/December 1983

ISBN: 0-515-06262-6

Jove books are published by The Berkley Publishing Group,
200 Madison Avenue, New York, N.Y. 10016. The words
"A JOVE BOOK" and the "J" with sunburst are trademarks
belonging to Jove Publications, Inc.

PRINTED IN THE UNITED STATES OF AMERICA

Chapter 1

It was springtime in the Rockies. So the jaybirds were screaming, the loco weeds were sprouting, and half the white women in the state of Colorado were acting mighty strange.

The one in bed with Longarm that Sunday morning nudged him lovingly in the gut with her elbow and sobbed, "Oh, my God, we have to get you up, Custis!"

Longarm opened one eye, stared morosely at the slit of cold gray light under the drawn window shade, and said, "Well, you're a pretty little thing and I've always been a good sport. But can we go back to sleep again after? It can't be six o'clock yet and this is the only day in the week my fool boss lets me sleep late."

She nudged him again, harder. "I'm not talking about your pride and my joy, alas," she told him. "I just remem-

1

bered that pesky Irish gal is due to arrive any minute. I told her to get here early this morning. That was before I knew you were back in town, of course."

The widow woman sat up in bed, allowing the covers to fall away from her Junoesque upper story. Longarm stared up at her with undisguised admiration. "Now that you mention it, I *am* sort of rising to the occasion, honey. Lay your pretty head back down by mine and tell me why company is coming, while we come."

But as Longarm reached for her, she slid out of bed and headed for the duds she'd left on the dresser at a more romantic moment in their lives. Longarm watched wistfully as she proceeded to stuff her considerable charms inside a modest calico housedress. He sighed and asked, "Who in thunder is this Irish gal we're jawing about, and how come she or any other civilized she-male would be up and about at this ungodly hour?"

"Molly is my cleaning woman," the widow woman said. "I told her I meant to start my spring-cleaning this morning. I clean forgot about it when you showed up on my doorstep last night, you horrid, horny thing!"

Longarm started to argue, but he knew it was no use. It was greenup time, and no man born of mortal woman was about to convince *any* mortal woman that the world wouldn't end if spring-cleaning didn't start smack on time. He propped himself up on his elbow and reached for his hickory shirt on the bedside chair to fish out the smoke and matches a human being needed to wake himself up at the crack of dawn. But somewhere a woodpecker was tapping on glass and the widow woman gasped, "Oh, my God, she's here! I'll carry her to the front parlor and try to keep her there till you can get dressed and slip out the back way!"

Longarm started to tell her how dumb that was, but she was already out the bedroom door and on her way downstairs. So he cursed, sat up, and proceeded to haul his own duds on as he pondered the mysterious thought processes of womankind.

For such a warm-natured gal, the widow woman didn't know beans about avoiding the gossip she seemed so worried about. If she meant to start her own spring-cleaning this morning, it was a simple fact of tribal custom that every other woman on Sherman Avenue would be at the same fool chore. So if it had been up to Longarm, he'd have made his hopefully discreet exit by way of the *front* door. A full-dressed gent wearing a sober expression had an even-money chance of striding down the front walk without appearing on the society pages of the *Denver Post*. But sneaking half a block along the back alley with half the gals in the neighborhood beating rugs in their backyards was going to cause comment for certain.

He had no choice. As he dressed he could hear the widow woman and her cleaning woman moving along the hallway downstairs. The gal who'd just leaped out of bed to avoid his embrace was chattering away too loud and too innocent as she herded the Irish gal to the front of the house. He rose, resisted the impulse to stomp his stovepipe boots to a better fit, and strapped on his cross-drawn gun rig before donning his frock coat and pancaked Stetson. He didn't light the cheroot gripped between his teeth as he eased out of the bedroom. The cleaning woman would likely wonder about it if she smelled three-for-a-nickel tobacco as she dusted later.

Longarm moved down the back stairs on the balls of his feet while the gals up front chattered like magpies about lamp chimneys, carpets, and other critters in need of purification after a long hard winter. He cracked the back door, peered out, and when he saw that no Cheyenne were scouting the widow woman's backyard, made a beeline for the back gate.

He made it to the alley without being spotted—he hoped. After that it got more complicated. As he moseyed down the alley between the trash cans and ash barrels, an ugly old gal came out her back door, dragging a rug by the tail with one hand as she brandished a club in the other. She gaped at Longarm as if he'd been walking on water instead of the gritty cinders of the alley. He smiled pleasantly at her and ticked the brim of his Stetson to be polite. She just went on staring at him, suspicious as a homesteader regarding a cowhand with a pair of wire cutters in his hands.

It got worse. Longarm was spotted by at least a dozen neighborhood gals of all sizes, shapes, and charms. One old gal, not bad looking, had thought she could make it to the outhouse in her kimono at such an early hour. When she spied Longarm smiling over the back fence at her she spooked like a mustang full of loco weed and ran back to her house, yelling foolish things about a tramp prowling in the alley.

Longarm sighed and started walking faster. He knew that before the morning was half over his mysterious comings and goings would be the talk of the whole infernal neighborhood. He hoped they wouldn't be able to say just whose back door he'd slipped out of. But since the widow woman was the most likely suspect, some mean mouth was sure to put two and two together and, worse yet, blab about it for a month of Sundays.

He saw with relief that he was approaching the end of the alley. There was a box dray and a team of mules parked behind the corner house, almost blocking the narrow alley. As Longarm worked around the obstruction, talking polite to the mules to avoid surprising them, he idly read the new gilt lettering on the side panels of the dray. They informed him that Mulligan & Sons cleaned cesspools cheap. He saw no sign of Mulligan or his sons. As he made it around the far side he glanced over the fence and saw the back door of the big brownstone house was open. It looked like a fancy enough house to have indoor plumbing and a cesspool.

Denver was getting mighty civilized these days. When Longarm had first seen the town, right after the War, it had been a roaring little gold camp along Cherry Creek. But that corner house was fancy enough to grace New York or even Frisco.

4

Longarm lit the cheroot he was still gnawing and stepped out on the side street leading back to Sherman Avenue, where he'd have been in the first place if women weren't so sneaky. A blue-uniformed beat copper swung the corner, eyed Longarm thoughtfully, then, recognizing him as a fellow lawman, said howdy.

Longarm pointed at the big corner house he'd just come out from behind and said, "Howdy, Nolan. You wouldn't know who lives in that fancy barn, would you?"

"Sure I would," Nolan said. "That's the Tabor mansion. But Silver Dollar Tabor ain't home at the moment. He's gone up to Leadville to scout a new strike. I know because he asked us to keep an eye on his place whilst he was outten town. Why do you ask, Longarm?"

Longarm frowned thoughtfully. "Just nosy, I reckon. Can we assume old Silver Dollar left his house servants in command of the post in his absence?"

The copper shook his head. "Hell, if he hadn't took his cook and butler with him to man the defenses of his Leadville house he'd have hardly asked us to keep an eye on *this* one, would he? What's going on, Longarm? I know you of old, and you've got that deer-stalking look in your eye again."

"I'll tell you what, Nolan," Longarm said. "Why don't you mosey around the front door and see what happens when I go in the back? I may be just mean-natured, but cover that front door from behind one of the elms out front and, while you're at it, get your gun out."

Nolan started to ask Longarm what on earth he was talking about, but Longarm had already turned and was heading back for the alley entrance. So Nolan started legging it the other way. He'd worked with Longarm in the past and, for a federal deputy, the big bastard was mighty neighborly about sharing credit with the local law.

The mules spooked a mite as Longarm swung in sight unexpectedly. He shushed and soothed them as he patted the near mule and tugged at its harness like an old pal.

Then, when the critters were calm again, he eased the back gate open and headed for the open rear entrance of the Tabor mansion. As he was mounting the steps, a burly man in coveralls came out the back door carrying a big stuffed sack over his shoulders like Santa Claus. Longarm didn't think he could be Santa Claus, so he drew his .44 and said, "Freeze. I won't say it twice."

The man with the sack gasped, swung the load off his shoulder to hurl at Longarm, groped for the gun in his hip pocket, and died still wearing a surprised expression as Longarm fired and sidestepped at the same time. The sack crashed loudly on the walk behind Longarm and silverware went tinkling in every direction as the thief subsided on the threshold with a duller thud. Longarm leaped over the bulky cadaver and crabbed to one side out of the doorway light as he charged into the unfamiliar house.

It was well he did so. For a gun muzzle blossomed unfriendly at the far end of the dark hallway and a bullet hummed through the space Longarm would have occupied had this been his first such appearance at a burglary in progress.

He returned the greeting with a .44-40 slug of his own. He couldn't tell who or what he'd hit, but it sure sounded noisy. There was a crash of metal and the slamming of a door up ahead. Longarm crabbed across to the far wall and slid along it through the gunsmoke until he spotted a form stretched out on the floor like a corpse. But as he got a better look at it he saw he'd shot a suit of armor off its base.

He had no idea why Silver Dollar Tabor wanted an antique knight in his fancy fool hallway, but he didn't think the tin man had fired at him, so he stepped over the armor and kept going until he came to a three-way choice of doorways.

Like most of the plush brownstones of Denver, the front entrance of this house led into a vestibule with big sliding doors on either side. One likely led to a dining room and

the other a front parlor. Longarm knew he'd have heard if
the burglar had run out the front entrance into Nolan's gun
sight. So that left two doors for Longarm to choose from.

He took a deep breath, stood to one side, and slid open
the door to his right. He cursed when he saw he'd opened
the parlor door. It was empty and a blind alley. That meant
his gun-toting burglar had ducked into the dining room—
and the dining room was surely connected to the kitchen
and, worse yet, the back door.

Longarm started to step into the dining room, thought
better of it, and ran back along the hall, leaping over the
suit of armor.

The thief he'd nailed still lay in the open rear exit. Longarm didn't pay him any mind. He'd known from the way
the rascal fell that he'd never bother anyone again. It was
more important to make sure that the one or more who'd
fired on him didn't make it out of the neighborhood. Tracing
a stolen and repainted dray could be a long tedious task,
and he wasn't paid to do detective work for the city of
Denver.

He charged out the rear door, crabbing to one side again
and running along the flower beds edging the walk. Beyond
the gate he heard a whip snap, followed by the pounding
of hooves as the mule team drove off.

But Longarm had thought ahead. So he didn't run out
the gate like a greenhorn. He cut across the yard to where
a lady made of terra-cotta was pouring water into a corner
lily pond. He used the waist-high statuette as an improvised
stepladder and rolled over the back wall well clear of the
gate. So the bearded gent covering the gate from the front
seat of the new teamless dray with a puzzled expression and
a .45 S&W looked even more surprised as Longarm snapped,
"Drop it!" When he didn't, Longarm fired a round into his
chest, then shot him again for luck as he rolled off the seat
and landed on his head between the empty traces of his
stalled dray.

Longarm jumped down off the garden wall and walked

over to survey the damage, reloading on the way. As he rolled the second corpse over with his boot, the copper, Nolan, came to join him, gun drawn.

"What in the hell is going on, Longarm?" he called out. "I just seen a team of mules go lickety-split across Sherman Avenue and, seeing as all the shots were coming from back here . . ."

"I told you to cover the front," Longarm cut in, adding in a friendlier tone, "I reckon it don't matter now. It was me as unhitched the mules from the dray, before I went in. I put one on the ground at the back door. This other one slipped by me in the innards of that big old house. But, as you see, he didn't get far. I reckon Silver Dollar must have told lots of folks he figured to be out of town a spell."

Nolan looked at the lettering on the dray, whistled, and said, "Hey, that was pretty slick of 'em! Had I come by and seen what I thought was cesspool cleaners working out back, I'd have likely just kept walking."

Longarm nodded. "That's why they painted that sign on the dray, most likely. They meant to carry off everything of value in the house in it. As it is, there's a silver service all over the backyard and a suit of armor with some interesting new dents and at least one bullet hole. But, all in all, I'd say we minimized the damage some, between us."

"*Between us?* That's mighty generous of you, Longarm. But how in hell did you get wise to 'em?" Nolan asked.

Longarm saw some heads peering over backyard fences at them now, and a couple of menfolk had even stepped out into the alley to stare at a cautious distance. Longarm said, "It's spring-cleaning time. Our sneaky burglars forgot that cesspools are cleaned just *before* everyone opens all the windows to air their houses, not *after!* Besides that, it's Sunday. Housewives are allowed to break the Sabbath during a national emergency like spring-cleaning, but cesspool cleaners have to have a plumber's license, and no licensed business is allowed, by Denver law, to stoop to trade on the Lord's day."

"Suffering snakes, that's true!" the Denver copper gasped. "But I'd forgot the blue laws, seeing as so many businessmen in town pay little heed to 'em!"

Longarm shrugged. "Well, it's only natural for a saloon or a whorehouse to break the Sabbath, and I reckon the law winks at a pharmacy, a funeral parlor, or other needful business staying open on Sunday. But it struck me sort of queer that gents would be cleaning out a cesspool when the law says we should all be praying or inviting relatives over to Sunday dinner. How are we going to word your report so's you'll get your due share of the glory, Nolan?"

The copper shot him a grateful look and said, "You're a real pal to put me in for so much as an assist, Longarm. Like I said, you did all the smarts and all the shootings."

Longarm shook his head. "Back up and let's go over that again, old son. Said sounds of gunplay will doubtless have a mess of other law—and reporters—arriving any infernal minute. So we'd best get our story straight. As I recall, we met out front as I was walking to—uh—church. You knowed me to be law, so you asked me to help you check out a mighty suspicious cesspool cleaning operation, right?"

"If you say so. What happened then, Longarm?"

"Hell, don't you remember? You covered the house in front and sent me around to scout the back. I went down to the far corner and walked the whole length of the alley to come in from an unexpected angle, likely making some of the gals beating carpets out back sort of wonder, but a man has to do his duty. Anyway, as you suspicioned, the so-called cesspool cleaners were rascals and we had to shoot it out with 'em, right?"

"Longarm, I never shot nothing out with nobody."

"Sure you did. Don't be so damned modest, Nolan. Don't you *ever* want to make sergeant? I'll tell you what, let's split the glory even. I'll take credit for the one in the doorway and you got the one who got past me, here. I'd let you have both, but, to tell the truth, I've a reason for wanting the *Post* to print me up as having a good excuse for being in

9

these parts this particular morning."

They shook on it, and a little while later Nolan was telling the tale to some other coppers and a carriage full of reporters who'd arrived on the scene, just as Longarm had predicted.

Longarm made sure some of the widow woman's neighbors, who had by now screwed up the courage to approach within earshot, heard his noble reasons for creeping down their alley earlier that morning. Then, as the sun was up for the day by now, Longarm said *adios* to all concerned and headed on up Sherman Avenue with a relieved expression. It was still too early for a white man to be up on a Sunday morning, but he was wide awake now, and Henry's down by the stockyards might be open despite the blue laws.

He didn't make it. He knew his boss, Marshal Billy Vail, lived farther along Sherman Avenue, but in his anxiety to protect the widow woman's reputation—and seeing it was his day off anyway—he'd forgotten it entirely until he heard his name called from the front porch of the Vail house.

Marshal Billy Vail was older, shorter, and fatter than Longarm. At the moment he wore shirt-sleeves and a harried expression as he came down the walk to greet his tall deputy. Vail said, "I figured you might be in the neighborhood, Longarm. Just heard the dulcet tones of a .44-40 in the distance. I hope you didn't shoot that widow woman my wife says a child your age shouldn't mess with."

Longarm chuckled and said, "She ain't all that older than me—and, as far as I could tell, we parted friendly. Me and a Denver copper named Nolan just shot it out with some burglars at the Tabor mansion. Guess who won. Don't worry, boss, I fixed it so Denver gets to do all the paperwork."

The older lawman rolled his eyes heavenward. "I might have known you can't even visit a lady without gunplay," he sighed. "Let's set on the steps a spell, Longarm. I'd invite you inside, but my old woman has gone loco. Have you ever figured out why women get like that every damn greenup?"

Longarm followed him to the steps, wondering what he

10

wanted, as he said casually, "Don't try to figure it out, Billy. You're a man. No man has ever been able to figure why robins nest in apple trees and human she-males all decide to clean house on the same spring day."

They sat down together. Longarm's smoke was down to a stub that endangered his heavy moustache, so he snuffed it out and offered Vail a cheroot as well as he lit up again. Vail said he was too concerned with his dignity to smoke such cheap tobacco and fished out his own nickel-a-round cigar. He waited until they were both blowing blue clouds toward the deserted, elm-shaded avenue before he spoke. "The reason we're talking here and now is to save the taxpayers of these United States some money and my world-weary eyes your usual excuses for showing up late come tomorrow morning."

Longarm looked innocent and said, "Hell, Billy, I'm sure I showed up on time at least one or two Monday mornings this season."

Vail snorted. "Bullshit. You've been known to show up on time on *payday,* old son, but blue Monday ain't the day we expect you at the federal building before nine-thirty or later. So, as long as I have you at my mercy, you lazy rascal, I may as well give your your chores for the coming cold gray dawn."

"That sounds fair, boss. If I already know what you want me to do tomorrow, I won't have to bust a gut getting to the office in my usual punctual manner. What's up?"

"I have two important jobs," Vail said. "Being as you're only one of my deputies, I'll let you pick which one you want. We have to deliver a federal prisoner for a hanging, and we seem to have us a town-taming to tend to."

Longarm blew a thoughtful smoke ring and said, "I'll take the town-taming. I've been to a couple of hangings."

"You've always been a sentimental cuss, Longarm. But you'd best hear me out before you decide which job you want. Escorting the prisoner to his well-deserved hanging is a simple chore that shouldn't take more'n a few days of

11

your valuable time. The rascal murdered an Indian agent in the Cherokee Strip, but he had no fight left in him when Smiley and Dutch picked him up the other night in a cathouse by the Burlington Yards. He's on ice and wearing irons in the federal lockup across town. All you'd have to do would be to deliver him to the hangman at Fort Smith, get a receipt, and come on home. It's not like you'd have to watch the execution. They can string him up without our help, once we deliver the son of a bitch."

Longarm grimaced and said, "I'd still be the one as led him to the gallows. I don't mind shooting an owlhoot. I don't even mind watching one hang, if I've reason to be sore at him. But a long-drawn-out train ride with a total stranger who's fixing to die can be sort of mournful. Tell me about the other case."

Vail sighed. "It's a mean one," he told his deputy. "The Justice Department has ordered us to investigate a bucket of snakes up Custer County way. The county seat's a bitty trail town called Scott's Wells. Do you know the place?"

Longarm nodded and said, "Some. Passed through it one time when I was riding with Captain Goodnight. Never paid it much mind, for it ain't the sort of trail town anyone pays much mind to. As I recall, it's a watering stop on the Goodnight Trail, in the foothills of the Front Range. Wasn't much action there. The locals seemed to be some sort of foreign folk, with mighty dim views on the usual amusements of cowhands passing through. They had half a dozen churches and hardly a saloon worth mention. You say this town needs *taming*, Billy? Hell, if Scott's Wells was any tamer, ever'body in town would have to be dead and buried."

"That's just what's been happening in Scott's Wells!" Vail exclaimed. "At the rate things are going, the population of the graveyard will soon outnumber the folk still up and about their otherwise dull business. You're right about 'em being uninteresting foreigners. Most of the settlers seem to be Scotch immigrants. The reason they have so much churches and so few saloons is that they take their hellfire-and-damnation religious notions serious. They talk funny, too."

Longarm thought, nodded, and said, "I do recall, now, that the folk in that trail town had Scotch brogues. I was too anxious to ride on to inquire into their history. How come a mess of Scotchmen all wound up in that one tedious place, Billy? Do you know?"

Vail said, "Sure. A British cattle syndicate sent 'em over to raise some sort of Scotch beef critter on the High Range. But it didn't work so good, betwixt the Scotch cows refusing to thrive on short grass and hungry Injuns eating the ones as did. The British investors lost interest and pulled up stakes."

"You mean they just stranded the poor greenhorns they sent to herd Highland cattle?"

"Oh, they made out all right in the end. Some filed homestead claims whilst others took to raising sensible long-horns or went into some other business in and about the one serious town in the county. But that's ancient history, Longarm. The killings are recent, and the only part the Justice Department is interested in."

Longarm frowned. "Hold on. Homicide is a local offense if it happens in an incorporated county. How come Justice wants us looking into Custer County? What's the matter with the sheriff up that way?"

"He's dead," said Vail. "Sheriff Angus MacMillan was bushwhacked a couple of weeks ago, not long after he replaced a Sheriff MacTavish, who'd been stabbed in the back by a person or persons unknown. They don't *have* a sheriff now. Nobody wants the job. They used to have a town marshal, but he resigned and left for other parts after someone sent him a note threatening his wife and kids."

Longarm whistled softly and said, "Scott's Wells must be a more interesting town than me and Captain Goodnight ever took her for. But I still fail to see the *federal* angle, Billy. Ain't it usual for local governments to appeal to state

13

or territorial authorities when things get out of hand?"

Vail nodded. "It gets even stickier," he went on. "Nobody has asked for help from anyone. The political powers that be, this side of the Big Muddy, don't want jurisdiction as a gift. It's an election year, remember?"

Longarm pursed his lips. "I follow your drift. The near-at-hand machine hates to risk losing votes, and folks tend not to vote for folks who send in outside lawmen uninvited. How does Scott's Wells vote—Republican or Democrat?"

"Nobody knows. That's another reason we have to investigate the situation up there, Longarm. You see, both the Democrats and Republicans have sent precinct workers up to Scott's Wells to organize some voting for this fall. But nobody would talk to the workers from either party. Then somebody run 'em all out of town with some well-aimed shots across their bows."

Longarm took another drag on his cheroot, blew another thoughtful smoke ring, and said, "Shooting up the law and preventing folks from voting *can't* be constitutional, Billy. Is anything else going on up there that I might want to hear about?"

Vail sighed. "You know as much as I do now. I told you it was a bucket of snakes. If Justice knew the whole picture they wouldn't be asking me to send men to investigate the spooky doings, would they?"

"I reckon not. But let's simmer down on the plural, boss. You know I like to work alone."

Vail shook his head. "Not this time, Longarm," he said. "I just got done telling you it's a bucket of snakes. We don't know who's doing what to whomsoever up in Custer County. You'd be riding in blind, with no notion as to who you could trust. The whole population seems mighty surly to outsiders, and at least one of 'em has to be a cold-blooded murderer. Notice I said *murderer*, not a stand-up-and-be-counted killer. I don't doubt you could handle a foreign gunslick or two, for I've seen you do it. But Sheriff MacTavish was stabbed in the back in the dark, and Sheriff

MacMillan was shot in the back the same way. So I'm ordering you to take at least two deputies along, if only to cover your fool *back*. Who do you want from the team?"

Longarm started to argue, but he changed his mind. On rare occasions old Billy Vail could be talked out of a foolish notion, but not when his pudgy jaw was set the way it was. So Longarm shrugged and said, "Hell, you pick 'em. You know I don't want a backup team, and if anyone working with me gets killed I want to leave you all the credit."

Vail had been braced for an argument. He looked much happier as he punched Longarm's shoulder jovially and said, "There you go, old son. It's about time you started minding your elders. Meet Smiley and Dutch at the office tomorrow, and for God's sake try to get there before noon. I'll have Henry type up your orders, travel vouchers, and such ahead of time, so the three of you can be on your way fast and arrive in Scott's Wells long before sundown."

A she-male voice called something from inside the house in a tone of frustration. Vail got to his feet, muttering, "Damnation. Them rugs surely could have survived another day without my whupping them half to death. But you know womankind when they get like this. We'll talk about your hotel accommodations and how I can keep in touch with you up there when we meet at the federal building tomorrow, all right?"

Longarm got to his own feet, said something noncommittal, and they parted friendly. As Vail went in to help his wife prepare the house for a visit from Queen Victoria, Longarm headed downtown.

A block away, Longarm consulted his pocket watch and groaned at the thought of being up this early on his only day off in the week. Then he grinned to himself as he looked on the bright side. He was up and about with the whole day ahead of him. Billy Vail would be stuck helping his wife with the spring-cleaning all day, so how was *he* to know what his deputies were doing?

Longarm didn't know where Smiley and Dutch were at

15

the moment—and, better yet, neither he nor Vail had any way of getting in touch with them before Monday morning. So Longarm started walking faster. He could easily make it to the Burlington Yards before the morning cattle train pulled out. A man didn't need infernal travel vouchers if he bought drinks regular for the good old boys around the railyards. So he'd kill an otherwise dull Sunday and make it to Scott's Wells long before his fussy boss and those other tedious deputies could even miss him.

Chapter 2

The first thing Longarm learned about Scott's Wells as he bought a schooner of needled beer for the Burlington Yard boss at Henry's near the track was that Scott's Wells was really spelled Scots Wells, no matter what the Justice Department had on paper. It was pronounced the same way, but it meant Scottish Wells rather than some wells belonging to a gent named Scott. The yard boss told him that the county seat was still on the Goodnight Trail, but not on the railroad. "The county seat's about an hour's ride from the flag stop at Rabbit Wash, Longarm," the yard boss added. "I doubt there's a livery there. But we can just as easy let a pony ride free as we can you."

Longarm had already picked up his McClellan saddle, Winchester, and possibles at his furnished digs across Cherry Creek. "I hadn't planned on carrying a mount along from Denver," he said, "but you likely know the place better than me. As a matter of fact, I never heard of Rabbit Wash. How come the train stops there instead of the county seat?"

The yard boss swallowed a slug of needled beer and wiped his moustache before he replied. "We don't stop anywhere in Custer County unless the stationmaster flags us down or we have some freight like yourself to drop off in Rabbit Wash. About the only time the Burlington does much business there is during roundup time. All the beef shipped from the spreads in that neck of the woods is driven to Rabbit Wash to be poked aboard. The town itself, if you want to call it a town, is even smaller than Scots Wells. It wouldn't even be there if the Burlington hadn't needed a cow loading stop in Custer County when they laid the tracks a few years back."

Longarm frowned thoughtfully and asked, "How come they didn't run the rails through the county seat, then? It's all the same rolling prairie from the foothills east. I'm no railroad surveyor, but I reckon I'd have laid the tracks less inconvenient."

The yard boss shrugged and said, "The front office back East would know better than me why they avoided Scots Wells. Meanwhile, if you don't aim to *walk* from the flag stop to the county seat, you'd best find a pony sudden. For the only way-freight I can offer you a free ride aboard will be pulling out in less than an hour."

Longarm nodded, told Henry to refill his pal's stein, and picked up his gear. He lugged it to the nearest livery on Nineteenth Street and selected a sensible-looking buckskin mare with a silly name. Then he saddled old Petunia up and rode her back to the railyards.

Forty-three minutes later they were on their way north, with Petunia riding up front in an empty cattle car and Longarm drinking coffee with the brake crew in the rear.

None of the train crewmen could say just why the Burlington had gone the long way around Scots Wells. Most of them had never even heard of the place and those who had didn't know anything about it. They thought somebody named Scott owned some wells there, too. So the trip was mighty tedious, but at least it was fairly short.

They made an unscheduled stop that afternoon to drop Longarm and Petunia off at Rabbit Wash. Longarm led the buckskin from the loading ramp by her reins as he sized up the flag stop. The Denver yard boss had told them true. Rabbit Wash consisted of a block-long main street fronting on the more impressive railroad siding's water tower and stock pens. He saw no station, let alone a stationmaster, but an old goat in faded denim and a railroad cap moseyed over to ask why the train had stopped.

Longarm explained and identified himself, adding, "Before I head off to the county seat, who do I see here in Rabbit Wash who would be able to tell me something about Scots Wells?"

The old switchman shrugged. "The newspaper gent over to the *Custer County Clarion* would likely be more sober at this hour than our one-man police force. But I can tell you all you need to know about Scots Wells, pard. Don't go there. Them furriners is all crazy to begin with, and they're having a *feud,* besides!"

Longarm said he hailed from West-by-God-Virginia and knew all about feuds. Then he led Petunia along the street until he saw the newspaper office. He tethered her out front and went inside. A dishwater blonde who would have looked better without the granny specs she was wearing looked hopefully at him from behind a counter dividing the front from the printing establishment behind her. When he said he was a lawman, not an advertiser, she sighed and called a fat man covered with printer's ink and a once-white shirt out from behind the press. He answered to the handle of Silas Redford and was the owner and operator of the *Custer County Clarion*.

Longarm asked what they'd been printing of late about the odd goings-on over in Scots Wells.

Redford looked uneasy and said, "Nothing. It ain't healthy to mention the Campbell or MacMillan factions in print or even by word of mouth. Both sides are surly as hell, and I'm a printer, not a gunslick."

Longarm nodded. "There's nobody listening in but this pretty lady here, Mr. Redford," he said. "We know something ornery is going on. You have to know more about it than I do, for I don't know beans."

Redford hesitated, then turned to the blonde. "You run along and mayhaps drink some tea or something for a spell, Nancy," he said. "I won't need you for twenty minutes or so—hear?"

Nancy nodded silently, put on her sunbonnet, and left them to their man talk. When she'd gone, Silas Redford explained, "She only works here, and the less a woman knows, the less she can gossip about it. Do I have your word this is a privileged conversation, Deputy Long?"

"You do, sir. I hardly ever gossip, and I'm assuming to start with that you folks here in Rabbit Wash ain't involved in the Scots Wells feud."

Redford nodded and said, "You're assuming right. You'd have to be a crazy Scotchman to understand it in full. But, from the little anyone's told us real Americans, it's some sort of war left over from the old country. Back in Scotland, it seems, the MacMillans and the Campbells used to make a habit of killing one another every chance they got. Old habits must be hard to break."

"So I've heard," Longarm agreed. "The feuding and fighting in them Highlands must have been a caution. But let's back up a mite. I know the last sheriff shot in the back mysterious was named MacMillan. Which side was the late Sheriff MacTavish on?"

"Oh, he was a Campbell," Redford said. "As I understand it, both the clans Campbell and MacMillan are big outfits, with branches bearing different surnames. A clan is more like a tribe than a proper family. So some Campbells are named MacTavish, Burnes, Burnett, Denoon, Hawes, Loudoun, MacArthur, MacDermid, MacIvor, MacKellar,

Thompson, and so on. Look out for Gordie Thompson, the ramrod of the Double C. He's mean as hell."

"I will," Longarm said. "Do these MacMillans hide behind other names, too?"

Redford nodded and said, "They do. I don't know them all. The MacMillans hold the foothills farther west and are even harder to talk to. But some go by the names Baxter, Bell, or Bethune. Angus Bethune, who runs the Double M, is an ornery son of a bitch, too. Some say it was him as stabbed MacTavish in the back and started the feud up again. But, in all fairness, Angus Bethune is known more for gunplay. He's never been too sneaky about making his displeasure known."

Longarm sighed. "Well, at least the *brands* are easy to remember. Are those the two main spreads these mysterious clansmen ride for?"

Redford nodded. "They're the only spreads there *are* around Scots Wells. Anyone else would be asking for trouble if they tried to run a single cow on Campbell or MacMillan grass."

"Now that's more like the feuds I've dealt with in other parts, say, Lincoln County," Longarm said soberly. "They may be fussing about Scotch history as an excuse, but it looks like a plain old range war from here."

Redford shook his head. "It's not a range war. The two clans divided up the range fair and square when the British cattle syndicate pulled out a spell back and left the county to former employees. Those Highland Scotch are surly, but Calum MacMillan and Duncan Campbell shook on it. And, next to a good grudge fight, there's nothing a Highlander values more than his given word."

Longarm looked sincerely puzzled as he fished out two cheroots, offered Redford one, and waited until they'd both lit up. "I'm missing something," he said when they were both drawing smoke. "If these Scotch families came over here together working for the same cattle syndicate, divided

21

up the range neighborly, and managed to get along tolerable until recent, what in the hell do you reckon their infernal feud is *about?*"

"That's easy," Redford said. "It was the killing of Sheriff MacTavish. Up until then, the two sides got along tolerable, as you say, but they never really liked each other. Then MacTavish was murdered and replaced by a MacMillan. So some Campbell must have suspected dirty work at the crossroads and shot the MacMillan. Now there's no sheriff at all and both clans are forted up and braced for a showdown. See?"

Longarm shook his head. "No, I don't see. What evidence was there that the first sheriff, MacTavish, was murdered by a MacMillan?"

Redford said, "The killer left a message. It was engraved on the old Highland dirk someone left sticking out of his back. I didn't see it, and wouldn't have been able to read it if I had. But I hear the Campbells are keeping it as a memento. There was something inscribed in Gaelic on the blade. Whatever it was, it made the Campbells mad as hell."

Longarm blew a smoke ring. "I don't read Gaelic, neither," he said, "but I'd sure admire a look at that murder weapon when I ride over. Who did you say has it?"

"Duncan Campbell, the chief of the clan. Do yourself a favor and stay the hell away from old Duncan. He's crazy as a bedbug and he don't like outsiders."

"That's *his* problem," Longarm said. "I'm the law. Are all the folk in Scots Wells Scotch lunatics?"

"No, some of the towns folk are sensible Americans, like us. But the Scotch outnumber everyone else and run the county. That is, they did until they split into these two warring camps."

Longarm examined the tip of his cheroot thoughtfully and he mused aloud. "Hmm, that explains someone running off political workers in an election year. The warring factions ain't about to vote on the same side, but they don't want nobody else swinging any elections before they see who's left after the feud. Who would you say figured to win?"

Redford grimaced and said, "If I could even make an educated guess the *Custer County Clarion* would be backing hell out of them. Both sides can field about the same number of guns. The Campbells have the edge on controlling the town itself. The MacMillans are dug in better in the rougher foothills to the west. To tell you the truth, I don't see how either side can wipe the other out entire. But, meanwhile, it's sure unsafe for just about everyone in Custer County. If you federal men are all that interested, why don't you do her the easy way, Deputy Long? If I was you I'd never ride alone into that hornet's nest. I'd carry along at least a troop of cavalry and knock their heads together until they acted more American!"

Longarm shrugged. "You ain't me and I ain't you. So I thank you for your words of cheer, and I'll do her my way."

He started to turn away. Then he remembered what the Burlington men had told him and asked Redford, "Say, while we're about it can you tell me how come the Burlington avoided Scots Wells, even before it got so feudsome over there?"

Redford nodded. "Sure I can. I said those crazy Scotchmen managed to get along with one another until recent. I never said they got along with anyone *else!* When the rail crews were coming this way, some riders from either the Double C or the Double M got liquored up one night and offered to fight any infernal Irishman on earth just for the hell of it. Most of the Burlington track-layers were Irish, of course, and as willing to fight as any Scotchman. But the Burlington is in the business of railroading, not staging bare-knuckles boxing matches. So . . ."

"That clears up one mystery," Longarm said. "But could you give me an educated guess as to which crazy Scotch outfit cut off their noses to spite their faces and drive their cows farther to market?"

Redford pursed his lips thoughtfully. "Nobody knows for

sure. Both Duncan Campbell and Calum MacMillan said at the time that it was a mighty dumb way to get a railroad station in Scots Wells. If you want just a guess, I'd give the edge to the Campbells on that one. They're frothing-at-the-mouth Calvinists, and most Irishmen are Roman Catholics, as you know. The MacMillans had even farther to drive their stock, and it's my understanding that they came from a part of Scotland where the Irish are considered distant relatives. But, for God's sake, don't quote me! Both chiefs said they'd have the hides of the boys who ran off the railroad crews if they ever found out who they might have been. That was before the feud, of course, when they still spoke to one another, at least on formal occasions."

Longarm fished his watch from his vest pocket, consulted it, and said, "Well, I'll likely find out more once I get there, and if I don't mean to camp on the prairie, I'd best ride. What's the best hotel over to Scots Wells?"

Redford looked incredulous. "Were you expecting to stay at a *hotel?* Lord have mercy, Deputy, there's nothing like a hotel in Scot Wells! There's business enough for two mighty small saloons, since the Campbells and the MacMillans won't drink together. But a hotel would go bust for sure."

"Well, I'll ask in both saloons," Longarm said. "Mayhaps some widow woman takes in boarders."

Redford frowned and said, "You can't drink in *both,* Deputy. Like I said, one is Campbell and one is MacMillan."

"Hell, I ain't neither, so why can't I drink and jaw where I like?"

Redford shook his head sadly. "You still don't understand, do you? Those loco Scotchmen don't trust outsiders to begin with. Once you favor either side with your business, the other will surely have you down as a likely enemy. Like the other American townsfolk over there, you have to patronize establishments run by one clan or the other. Once you've had a drink at the Thistlegorm or bought an apple at Baxter's grocery no Campbell will talk to you. It's the other way round if you set foot inside the Argyle Arms or buy tobacco from MacIvor's general store."

"How am I to talk to both sides, then?"

"You can't. Like I said, take some troopers. You're a fool to ride in alone." Redford shook his head solemnly.

The wagon trace to Scots Wells ran alongside the dry wash from which Rabbit Wash took its name. The buckskin mare turned out to be as good a trail mount as he'd figured when he inspected her lines at the Denver livery. But Longarm rode slowly, getting the lay of the land and keeping his eyes peeled. Somebody hereabouts made a habit of dusting government workers for fun or profit, and this was natural bushwhacker's country.

The wagon trace and wash wound in lazy bends through higher grassy swells. The greenup had the grass higher and lusher on the skyline than it would be later in the summer when the prairie reverted to a tawny carpet of summer-killed and grazed-down short grass.

Old Petunia seemed puzzled by the slow pace Longarm set. She was feeling frisky after being cooped up most of the day and would have loped to get the kinks out of her legs had Longarm let her have the bit. But he patted the side of her neck and soothed, "Easy, old gal. We'll get there before sundown, trotting, and it's generally a good notion to arrive without bullet holes in your hide. I'll let you run a spell as soon as we come to more open ground."

He reined in and added, "Right now we'd best slow to a *walk* while I consider that rise over to our north. Would you say it was natural for grass stems to move when the wind ain't blowing?"

Petunia was an old cow pony and, as she sensed the wariness of her ride, she pricked up her buckskin ears and moved under him with her own muscles ready to cut in any direction. He smiled thinly and said, "Damn, I knew you'd worked Indian country in your day, despite your dumb name.

Let's see, now—if we sort of ride up to the south rise like lost innocents looking for a landmark, we ought to have a better view of that rise to the north."

He reined her to his left and they started up the gentle rise at an angle. It didn't work. Somebody on the north rise didn't want them to get an overlook. Instead of waiting for Longarm to ride past, as planned by most backshooting sons of bitches, the sniper in the tall grass across the way let fly a round.

From the sound it made whizzing past, the bushwhacker was armed with a .75 buffalo rifle. He wasn't out to scare folks with such expensive ammunition. A .75 slug was meant to put a buffalo bull on the ground and leave a human head unrecognizable when and if it hit one.

Longarm threw himself from the uphill side of the saddle, casually taking his saddle carbine along as he pretended to be hit. Petunia, of course, spooked and ran off as Longarm rolled in the deep green grass until he lay prone with the Winchester trained on the far rise. He didn't fire. A drift of blue smoke hung above the skyline over that way, but you hardly ever hear *smoke* scream in pain when you put a bullet through it. Longarm lay doggo, hoping the bushwhacker would move closer to see if he was hit or just funning.

The yellow bastard wasn't about to come to see Longarm. Instead he fired again, despite the range and the poor view he had to have of the lawman down in the thick greenup. Longarm fired back as, this time, he saw the muzzle flash. Then Longarm was up and running toward the unknown as fast as he could move in his low-heeled army boots, downhill. He carried his Winchester aimed the way he was running, ready to fire from the hip. But as he crossed the sandy dry wash and started up the far slope he heard the sound of galloping hooves. He kept going, but muttered, "Shit!" for he knew Petunia was standing still and enjoying some lush short grass on the slope behind him. He made it to the top of the rise in time to spy a distant figure riding hell for leather toward the North Pole. Longarm lowered the muzzle of his Winchester. *That's a mighty sudden horse he's riding, old son,* he told himself. *But you can't say much for the sand in his craw.*

He turned to retrace his steps, wondering for the first time if old Petunia was going to be one of those pesky ponies a man had to chase.

She wasn't. She eyed him thoughtfully as she went on grazing, but she resisted the natural impulses of her kind as he walked over and regathered the reins, talking polite and patting her like a friend before he remounted. "Well, you've had some grass and that son of a bitch with the buffalo rifle has extended his diswelcome," he told the mare. "So what say we get on into town in time for supper?"

Now that he saw that nobody was joshing about the surly ways of the folk in these parts, Longarm abandoned the wagon trace and rode Petunia along the ridge lines of the rises to make things tougher for the bushwhackers. It took them longer that way, but as he spied a mess of church steeples in the distance and corrected their drift to the south, Longarm lit another smoke and told Petunia, "Maybe it's just as well we're coming in from an unusual approach. It might be sort of interesting to see who acts the least surprised to see us. There's no telegraph wire following the wagon trace, so nobody but that rascal with the .75 should be expecting us."

Chapter 3

The town of Scots Wells seemed a mite bigger now than it had when Longarm had passed through a few years back with Captain Goodnight and a mess of Texas cows. But that wasn't saying much. The unpaved main street ran about four Denver blocks north and south. Residential streets branching off east and west were little more than lanes. The many churches and such business establishments as there were in town were all near the main street. As Longarm rode along it, he saw—as he had of course never noticed the last time he'd been through—that the names over the doorways on either side of the street had taken sides even before the recent trouble. All the businesses on the east side of the main drag belonged to folks that Redford had identified as Campbell clansmen, while the west side of the street seemed to be MacMillan territory. The Thistlegorm and Argyle Arms saloons were placed not only on opposite sides of the street but a discreet block away from one another.

He rode down to the end of the main drag, where a small town square formed a lollipop end of the stem. Two churches glared at one another from opposing sides of the square. Longarm didn't have to read the lettering on the churchyard tombstones to guess that the folks buried to the east were Campbells, while the MacMillans planted their dead to the west. He wasn't too interested in the dead. That buffalo round hadn't been fired his way by a corpse.

The combined town hall and county courthouse, with sheriff's office and lockup attached, occupied the north side of the square, on what was likely neutral territory. He reined in, dismounted, and tethered Petunia out front before he went up the plank steps and knocked on the door.

Nobody answered. They'd likely knocked off for the day and gone home for supper. He moseyed along the walk to the entrance of the sheriff's office. Nobody was there, either. He peered in the window but didn't see much, as the shades were drawn.

A voice at his elbow said, "There's nobody in there, stranger. What do you want in Scots Wells?"

Longarm turned with a smile. "I'm Deputy U. S. Marshal Custis Long, and I'm looking for such law as you might have in these parts these days."

The man who'd approached him was as tall as Longarm, which meant he rose higher than most men his age, and dressed cow. He would have been nice looking if he didn't scowl so. "There isn't any law in Scots Wells right now," he said. "The goddamned Campbells bushwhacked such law as we had."

"So I hear," Longarm said. "You must be a MacMillan."

"That's close enough," the tall hand replied. "I'm Angus Bethune. We started out as MacDonalds, but we've always rode with Clan Millan. Nobody in the old country had any use for the damned Campbells."

Longarm remembered Bethune was one of the proddy gents Redford had warned him about. He put out his hand and said, "I'm sure glad I'm named Long, then."

Bethune didn't offer to shake. His right hand went on hovering like a hawk near the single-action hog leg he wore tied down and side draw. Longarm ignored the insult. "No offense, but you don't talk like a Scotsman, Bethune," he said.

The surly local snapped, "It's Scots, or Scottish, god damn it! If you have to say it, say it right. I talk American 'cause I was born and weaned American, but even I know better than to call anyone Scotch! There's Scotch whiskey and butterscotch candy, but there's no such thing as a Scotch *person*—and see that you don't never call me that again, hear?"

"I stand corrected," Longarm said. "Now that you've given me a lingo lesson, suppose you tell me where I can find someone who is in charge of things hereabouts. For the sun is sloping and my pony and me need to settle down somewhere if I'm to get an early start on my investigation come morning."

As they'd been standing there, a couple of other cowhands had drifted their way. Before Bethune could reply, one of them asked, soft and sort of shy, "Is there any help you'd be needing, Angus?"

Bethune contemplated Longarm as if he'd just noticed a horse turd on the walk and replied, "It's nothing I can't handle, Murdoch. I was just telling this Sassenach how much healthier he'd be if he forked that old buckskin nag and rode somewhere else."

Longarm sighed. "Now you've insulted Petunia, too. But before we have us a war, boys, you'd best hear me out."

"There's nothing we want to hear, Sassenach," Bethune said. "We know what needs to be done, and we don't need any outside help."

"Oh, shit, stop talking tedious. Anyone can see you must have at least a spoonful of brains, for you're standing sober

31

as me. I don't know what a Sassenach is, so I won't take it as dirty as it sounds. The point I'd make, if you boys would grow up and listen, is that running me off would be dumb as hell for several reasons. For one thing, I get surly when folks try to run me out of town. But, if that don't scare you, a couple of other federal deputies figure to stick their noses into your affairs as soon as my office notices I didn't wait up for them. If you think *I'm* hard to get along with, wait till you meet Smiley and Dutch!"

Bethune shrugged. "We can handle as many strangers as need be," he said.

Longarm shook his head in wonder. "I take it back. You *can't* have a spoonful of brains. You are talking to the U. S. government, friend. Don't you have enough trouble with them Campbell rascals?"

"We can handle them, too," Bethune said stubbornly.

"That ain't for me to say, Bethune. But I know the Justice Department better than I do anyone hereabouts, and you are just talking silly if you say you and them Campbells combined can take *us* on."

Bethune's eyes narrowed and his gun hand had tensed.

Longarm snapped, "Don't be an ass. Anyone can see it's three to one here, though I wouldn't bet on it if I were you. But even if you *can* take me out, my pards will just keep coming. And even if you get lucky as hell and manage to take out Smiley and Dutch, there's more where we all came from. Aside from the U. S. Army, if you *really* want to get silly, you hold your lands at the discretion of the U. S. Department of the Interior and ship your cows when and if the U. S. Department of Commerce says you can."

Bethune looked like he still needed some convincing. But a crusty voice with a pronounced burr rang out, "Angus Bethune, what are ye up to now, ye wee brainless bairn?"

They all turned to face a man in rusty black coming at them like a soldier on parade. He was older than all of them put together, but he was even taller than Longarm or Bethune. He was dressed like an American, in a sort of minister's or undertaker's suit, but one side of his black Stetson was pinned to the crown by a sort of silver badge with a sprig of holly tucked behing the clan badge like a plume.

Bethune looked nervous as he said, "Evening, Toshach. We were just telling this meddlesome stranger to mind his own business, is all."

"Och, were ye, now?" replied the old man in a frosty voice. He turned to Longarm and added, "I am Calum MacMillan, and it's for me to say who stays or goes in Custer County. State ye'r name and business, Sassenach. Ye other lads, be off with ye. I'll deal with this."

Bethune protested, "Toshach, the man is wearing a double-action .44 under that frock coat!"

But the old man snapped, "I said be off and I meant it, ye wearisome pup! Does any man here dare to say that the MacMillan himself can't handle any one man born of mortal woman?"

The bully and his pals shuffled off down the walk, grumbling, as old MacMillan turned back to Longarm and said, "Well?"

Longarm explained who he was and what he was doing in town. He felt like he was talking to a wooden Indian; the old chief stared silently at him until he'd finished. Then MacMillan said, "Aye, I knew sooner or later they'd send someone. Ye'r point is well taken that we'd probably be better off if ye finished your snooping and rode out unmolested. But talking is a thirsty business. So let us discuss the matter sitting doon in the civilized surroundings of the Thistlegorm!"

Longarm agreed. He left Petunia where she was and walked the short distance to the MacMillans' saloon with the old chief. As they passed people on the walk, Longarm noticed that they all greeted his guide as if he were Queen Victoria strolling the streets of London. Longarm didn't have to ask what a Toshach was. He already knew old Calum was the chief of the MacMillan faction. But as they approached the batwings of the Thistlegorm he asked the old Scotsman what a Sassenach was.

The Toshach smiled thinly and replied, "In the Gaelic, an Englishman. In practice, a Lowlander or anyone else wha's not a civilized human being."

"I knew it sounded dirty. I disremember what old country the Longs hailed from before they wound up in West-by-God-Virginia. I doubt they were Scotch. Oops, sorry—I meant Scottish."

"Och, dinna frush about such nit-picking, Deputy. A real mon of Gaidhealtachd couldna care less what a poor stranger who has no Gaelic calls him in English. Scotch and Scottish are both English words. We call *ourselves* Albannachs or, better yet Gaidheals, in the auld country."

"Do tell? From the way Angus Bethune carried on, I thought it was important," Longarm remarked.

The old chief waited until they were inside the saloon and seated at a corner table before he said with a sniff, "Och, poor Angus Bethune wouldna ken if he was called a two-headed calf in the language of his ancestors. None of the young ones have the Gaelic over here, I fear. Ye may have noticed he looks for fights."

"Well, I've met friendlier gents in my time," said Longarm. "But ain't it true he'd only have to cross the street and fight all them there Campbells, if he was serious about being the bully of the town?"

A waiter came over unasked and placed two schooners of what Longarm thought was flat beer on the table between them. The old man took a sip from his, sighed, and said, "That's refreshing. The reason Angus picked on ye is that I've forbidden him to pick a fight with yon Campbells. I've sent word to Duncan Campbell that I'm waiting on his word before we light the war crosses for once and all."

Longarm said that sounded reasonable and picked up his own drink. He let out a strangled gasp and wheezed, "Jesus Christ, you might have warned me that was straight spirits!"

34

The old man swallowed some more of his own drink as if he were sipping lemonade on a warm day. "Och, it's not spirits, mon. It's good malt liquor fra' Glenspey. They keep some for me here, knowing I've never been able to abide Yankee bourbon or, Laird preserve us, what they call Scotch whiskey in this country."

Longarm got his breath back, resisted the impulse to ask for some sissy chaser like gin or rye, and said, "Let's talk about this feud of yours. Are you saying it ain't official yet?"

"Aye, some of the younger gillies are spoiling for blood and slaughter, as ye just saw. But when I asked Duncan Campbell if he wanted peace or war, he denied giving orders for the murder of Sheriff MacMillan and said it was ourselves at fault, for striking the first blow with the killing of Sheriff MacTavish before declaring Fire and Sword."

Longarm figured he halfway understood the quaint way old MacMillan put things, so he didn't ask for further clarification about Scotch customs but took the bull by the horns and asked right out, "Would you tell me if you had ordered MacTavish killed?"

MacMillan looked insulted. "I would," he said. "It's the Campbells who have ever had the name for fighting underhanded. Ye can look it up in the histories of the clans, if ye like, and ye'll never find a word about the Proud MacMillans resorting to treachery."

Longarm took another sip of Highland lava, managed not to weep openly now that he was getting used to it, and said, "Someone put a mighty treacherous knife in the back of Sheriff MacTavish, though."

"Aye," the old man said, "and if he'd been a MacMillan he'd have gloried in it. It's no secret our clans have never been fond of one another. I recall a tale about a glorious cattle raid of our clan. We stole the grand cows of the Duke of Perth—a haughty auld bastard, he was—and we got away clean with his herd, too. But to show him who he owed the favor to, we left a scrap of MacMillan tartan tied to the gate of his empty cow pens."

Longarm repressed an impatient gesture. "That sounds like fun, sir. But can we get back to the stabbing of MacTavish in this particular century? I hear tell there *was* a message from your MacMillans writ on the blade of that dirk in Gaelic."

The old man grimaced and replied, "So the Campbell says. I asked auld Duncan to let me see the murder weapon. He refused. For all I know, the whole tale is a fairy story. I was oot at the Double M when the sheriff was murdered. For all I know he was stabbed wi' an ice pick."

"Was Angus Bethune out on your spread with you that night?" Longarm asked.

The chief frowned and hesitated. "Angus was where I *said* he was to be!" he finally replied. "I know ye're a stranger as well as a lawman, Long, so I won't take that the way Angus might. I'll tell ye mon to mon, the lad is not the sort who'd play Campbell tricks wi' a dirk in the dark. Ye saw for yersel' he's a bit of a bully. But ye also saw he didna hesitate to face a lawman doon in broad daylight."

"Yeah, I thought he was stupid, too. Before we change the subject, would Angus Bethune have any reason for killing MacTavish?"

"Och, of course he would! MacTavish was a Campbell and the Bethunes are MacDonalds, with even more reason to hate the False Argyles than us MacMillans. Ha' ye never heard of the Massacre of Glencoe, mon?"

"Did it happen recent?"

"Ay, it was aroond 1692, as I recall."

Longarm repressed a laugh. "I'll pass on that particular tale," he said. "You say yourself that old Angus don't know much more than me about your old country."

He took another sip of firewater without thinking, swallowed to get it the hell out of his poor mouth, and wheezed, "Let's see if I have it straight between us, sir. What you want me to tell Uncle Sam is that you don't want a war with them Campbells if they don't want a war with you?"

"Aye. But, as ye see, the underhanded creatures *do*, deny it as they will. For, if they didna want a feud, why did they kill our Sheriff MacMillan?"

"I mean to ask Duncan Campbell that when I talk to him," said Longarm. "Does he live here in town, sir?"

"Och, nae, he's hiding from us oot at his Double C, five miles ootside of town. Ye'll not want to ride out there after dark, mon."

"Why not? Do they go to bed with the chickens?"

"I dinna ken, for I've never spent the night under any Campbell's roof, in the auld country or over here. I do know they shoot at things that gae boomp in the nicht, though. They're expecting *us* to *attack*, ye see! Sae if a stranger were to ride on their land in the dark, unexpected . . ."

Longarm nodded. "Daylight does sound safer, now that I've met up with the sort of ranch hands you breed in these parts. Meanwhile, I'd best figure out where I'm to spend the night with my pony. It's early enough for me to drink and talk along the main street some, but I'd rather know where I was headed in advance, once I've had enough."

The MacMillan said, "Ye're welcome to sleep wi' clansmen here in toon. Anyone of Clan Millan I ask wi' be proud to put ye up."

Longarm thought, shook his head, and said, "That's mighty neighborly, sir, but I'd just as soon not appear to be taking sides till I know what side I'm on. No offense?"

The old man shrugged. "Aye, ye would have trouble getting within rifle range of the cowardly Campbell after spending a nicht under a MacMillan roof. Let me think . . . Och, I ken where ye could ask. There's a Sassenach spinster named Walker wha takes in traveling drummers passing through toon noo and again. I've noo idea wha' she charges, but I'll show ye her hoosie. It's near the square where we met. But finish yer drink first, mon. Ye've barely touched it."

Longarm sighed and said, "I can already feel what I have

touched, thanks, and I want to be able to get about under my own power for at least a few more hours. I'd be much obliged if you'd show me the way to that boardinghouse, sir."

The old man shrugged, reached across to pick up Longarm's still nearly filled schooner, and said, "Waste not, want not."

Then, as Longarm stared, bemused, old Calum Mac-Millan swallowed the whole thing at one gulp. He'd already polished off his own heroic draft, so Longarm was braced to catch him as they both stood up. But the old man looked as sober as a judge as he led the way outside again.

It was starting to grow dark now. MacMillan said, "It's this way," and started walking.

Longarm said, "Excuse me, sir, the square's up the other way."

MacMillan turned, frowned, and said, "Och, so it is. Come along then. We'd best bed ye doon. For I see ye're noo a mon wha can hauld his liquor."

As they started walking the right way, Longarm said, "I'm all right. I had the sense to stop when I tasted what was in them schooners."

The MacMillan laughed and reached up to loosen his tie. "Och, who do ye think ye're fooling, laddie? Anyone can see ye're reeling aroond like a loon."

"If you say so. You say this landlady's name is Walker?"

"Who's walking daft, ye mad drunken loon?" the old man replied, sitting down on the plank walk with a sad shake of his head. He added, "Tell me when we get to America, Maither, for it's seasick I am aboard this auld leaky tub, and that's a fact!"

Longarm stood over him and muttered, "Oh boy." Then, seeing a couple of townsmen headed his way, he waved them over and asked, "Are you gents on this gent's side?"

One said cautiously, "It's a Bell of Clan Millan I'd be. What's it to *you*, Sassenach?"

"Don't hand me that Sassy shit. Your Toshach needs

some help getting home, and I ain't headed that way."

The two clansmen exchanged glances. Then the other one sighed and said in a friendlier tone, "Aye, leave him to us. If ye've extended the hand of friendship to himself, forget what we called ye just noo."

Longarm said he knew the rules in Scots Wells and left them to get the old man home as best they were able.

He walked back to the square and got Petunia, who nickered wistfully at him, as if she'd been worried about his return. He led her instead of mounting up as he circled back toward the brighter lights. He told her, "There's a boardinghouse around here some damned place, Petunia. I'll have you in a stall with oats if ever I can find it. Remind me never to ask directions from a man who swallows whiskey by the quart again. I don't know where in thunder that Walker house is. It's got to be one of these frame houses, though."

He came to a cast-iron hitching post, looped the reins through the ring, and added, "Wait here. I'll just go up to that door and ask the folk inside where the Walker gal is."

He mounted the steps of the small frame house the hitching post went with. There was a light inside, but the glass of the front door was covered with lace curtains inside. He found a door pull and rang the front door, feeling foolish. But, what the hell, it was early.

He detected movement inside through the lace. Then the door opened and a mighty handsome gal was standing there in a dressing gown which matched her big blue eyes. Her long black hair was unpinned and down on either side of her heart-shaped face. She'd obviously not been expecting company. She stared up at Longarm and said—or asked, it was hard to tell—*"Bha, mas e bhur toil e?"*

Longarm sighed and said, "I can see I surely picked the wrong address, if I knew how to say so in your lingo, ma'am."

She switched to English as she replied in a delightful lilt. "Och, I didna ken ye were a Sassenach, sir."

Coming from her, the term didn't sound as insultful. So he smiled and explained, "Calum MacMillan told me there was a house hereabouts where I could hire a room, ma'am."

Before he could go on to explain further she said, "The Toshach sent ye to be given a *seomar?* Och, come inside, then. I'd be Fiona MacPhee, Mr.... ah...?"

"Long, ma'am, Deputy U. S. Marshal Custis Long. But before we get in more trouble, are you MacPhees Mac-Millans or Campbells?"

She laughed and asked, "Have ye never heard of the Fairy tribe of Clan Duffy, then?" "No, ma'am, I didn't even know the name Duffy was Scotch," he said. "Are you saying you're neither MacMillan nor Campbell?"

"MacPhee is a clan in its own right, I'll ha' ye ken. Come in. Come in and let me close the door. For, as ye see, my hair is doon."

"I got a mare out front as needs a room, too, ma'am," he said. "Can I run her around to yer stable?"

The pretty blue-eyed brunette said, "Aye, put yer wee beastie awa' for the nicht and I'll let ye in the back door. Ye'll find hay and oats as well as a water pump next to the stall me own creature is in."

Longarm said that sounded fair and left her to get his buckskin and lead the animal around to the back of the house. Other critters nickered at them in the dark. He struck a match, lit a candle stub on a window sill, and found Fiona's stable the way she'd said he would. So he unsaddled Petunia, rubbed her down with some handy sacking, and left her in an empty stall with some water and fodder before returning to the house across the backyard.

The gal must have expected him, for the back door popped open before he could knock. As she stood there in welcome, the light from the coal-oil lamp on the kitchen table behind her shone through her robe in a way that might have made Fiona blush had she seen what he was seeing.

As his own unmentionable parts began to rise to the occasion, Longarm told himself to behave. The little gal was fully dressed and had no way of knowing how the light peeked between her thighs like that, with her hemline near the floorboards. She led him inside and sat him down to table, saying, "I'll show you to your *seomar* after we have some tea and scones."

"I know what tea and scones is, ma'am," he said. "If this *seomar* is a room I'll take your word it's fine. I got to go out again and nose about town some before I turn in."

Fiona shook her head as she placed a dish of what looked like plain old army hardtack in front of Longarm and poured tea. "You'd not be safe on the streets after dark, I fear. Did no one tell ye of the feud?"

As she sat across from him he said, "That's what I'm here to study on, ma'am. I've already heard the MacMillan side. I figure I'd mosey down to the Argyle Arms and see what the Campbells have to say for themselves."

"After dark? Surely you jest, sir!"

"What's the joke, then? Don't the saloons stay open at night in these parts?"

"Och, they used to. But since the killings started no mon on either side would be mad enough to coom out of a doorway wi' the light at his back after dark! The Thistlegorm and the Argyle Arms will both be closed by now, I fear."

"Do tell? You don't fear it as much as me, ma'am. I'm on a tight old timetable and I was hoping to get some investigating over before my pesky boss noticed. Fortunately for my conscience and his peace of mind, I see there's no Western Union office here in Scots Wells. Would anything else be open at night?"

"Not at nicht. Not wi' the clans at feud," she insisted.

So Longarm settled down to inhale some tea and scones. He'd forgotten he'd missed supper until he tasted her baking and the good strong tea. He tried to go easy on the latter, for if he was meant to turn in early he didn't want to waste time counting sheep, and the tea was the kind that perked a man up. But he couldn't help sipping it to wash down the dry scones. As they sat there making small talk Longarm learned that Fiona lived alone. He asked if she was a widow woman, but she sighed and said she was an old maid. He grinned across the table at her and said, "If you're a spinster it must be by your own choice, ma'am."

She lowered her lashes and replied, "Och, away wi' your Sassenach gallantries, sir. It's a dried-up auld maid of twenty-four I am this nicht. I was engaged to wed Alasdair MacInnes, years ago, but while my father lived he opposed the match, and by the time himself died, Alasdair was wed away to another."

Longarm didn't have a good response for the old familiar story, so he didn't even try. It was still mighty early, damn it, and here he was stuck out in the middle of nowhere with nobody to make eyes at but an infernal virgin. He decided not to try that, either. Next to going to bed early with nothing to read, there was nothing more tedious than going to bed with an erection after working it up pointlessly.

By now the widow woman on Sherman Avenue would be finished with her fool spring-cleaning or, if she wasn't, that redhead at the Black Cat would be getting off about midnight, and it didn't look like she cleaned her own digs.

A million years went by and then all the tea and scones were gone and Fiona asked if he'd like to see his *seomar* now. He nodded, too polite to say, "Aw, hell, may as well." So they rose and she led him from the kitchen, holding a candle. He followed her upstairs, relieved to note that the candle wasn't strong enough to shine through her robe. He had enough on his mind right now.

On the second-story landing he looked out and saw that the lights along the main street were, in fact, all out. Folks sure turned in early in these parts. The only bright light he could see from there was a distant pinpoint, well outside town to the east. It looked more like a bonfire than the glow from some ranch-house window. Fiona saw it too and muttered in Gaelic. She sounded worried. He asked her what was up and she said, "I don't know for certain. It's the wrong hill. Here's the door to your *seomar*, Custis Long."

42

She opened the door and led him into a small, spartan, but clean and sweet-smelling bedroom. She placed the candle on the bed table and turned down the covers, saying, "The sheets are not linen, I fear, but the cotton is clean."

He sniffed the lavender scent rising from the soft-looking bed and said he liked cotton sheets better, anyway. Fiona moved to the window and looked out again at the distant flickering beacon. He waited an awkward moment before he cleared his throat and asked, "Ah, how much do Petunia and me owe you, Miss Fiona?"

She turned toward him with a puzzled look. "Owe? Och, what are ye talking aboot? Would ye insult a poor auld spinster by offering her silver when no silver has been asked?"

"I'm sorry, ma'am. I must say you're about the most neighborly lady I've run across since Rabbit Wash, though. It don't hurt me to pay my own freight, since Uncle Sam generally winds up paying me back."

She shook her head stubbornly. "Don't talk of silver alone wi' a woman. It's unseemly. Would ye like to go to bed noo?"

He couldn't think of anything better to do in such an uncivilized town, so he said he would. He expected her to leave, but she shut the door, snuffed out the candle, and, from the sound of whispering cloth, it sure seemed like she was taking her duds off.

As his eyes adjusted to the dim light coming in from the sky outside, he saw that she was getting into the bed as well. He blinked in surprise. Then he grinned and proceeded to shed his own duds, a lot faster than he'd originally planned.

Chapter 4

As Longarm slid between the sheets with her and took her naked body in his arms, Fiona pressed tight against him and sobbed, "Och, Custis, I'm so verra verra frightened."

He went on holding her, but made no further move and even drew back his rising erection from where it had started to snuggle as he pondered her words. There were spinsters and then there were spinsters. If she was trying to convince him she was a bashful virgin at a time like this, it was an insult to his intelligence.

On the other hand, it sure felt good to have her naked nipples against his chest like that, and if she didn't feel what was pressing against the lower part of her belly despite his best efforts to be modest, she was even dumber than he thought she took him for. He knew lots of gals liked to play kid games at times like these, so he kissed her a couple of times to keep her from saying anything else as he ran his free hand over her to sort of break the ice.

She felt good all over and she didn't act coy. As he parted her pubic hair with his gentle fingers and began to massage her between the thighs, Fiona opened her thighs and began to move her hips sensuously even as she repeated, "Och, I'm so scared!"

This was no time to tell a lady she was a born liar, so he kissed her some more and soothed, "Don't be scared, honey lamb. I'll be gentle. I know all about breaking in you virgin gals. For half the gals I go to bed with assure me of their chastity."

She groaned and said, "Och, put it in me, you fool! Who said I was a virgin? Would I be here if that were so, you great Sassenach loon?"

That made more sense than anything else she'd said of late. So Longarm rolled into the soft saddle of her wide-spread thighs and nudged his old organ grinder into place. She was already lubricating good and rose to meet his entering thrust, but as they got to know each other better she gasped and said, "Och, Laird have mercy! I see ye're great in every way! Easy noo, I'm not in practice, as I feel *ye* must be, and . . . Aye, that's bonny. That's—Och, that's *marvelous!* Poond me hard and make me forget the beacons on the hills aboot, for I'm ever sae frightened and . . . Aye, aye, do it hard and let's forget the madness oot in the nicht!"

Longarm didn't need her encouraging words, though they were flattering. For Fiona was younger and tighter built than the widow woman he'd missed spending Sunday with back in Denver. As he made love to the sweet little brunette in the sweet-scented bed, Longarm was glad spring-cleaning had left him unsatisfied. This was satisfaction indeed.

Fiona came ahead of him, begging for mercy, then came with him the second time. As they went limp in one another's arms, he kissed her throat and asked if she was still scared of him.

She held him closer, if that was possible, and crooned, "It was never yersel' I was afrighted by. Though, now that I feel ye inside me, I should have been. I'm sae glad

46

ye're a bonny lover, Custis. I was concerned ye might not be. I've never made love to a Sassenach before, ye see."

He didn't feel it was wise to comment that she'd obviously been in bed with more than one Scotsman in her time. But he couldn't help asking her, "If you were afraid I'd be a tedious lover, how come we wound up in bed so sudden, honey lamb?"

"Och, did ye noo say the MacMillan himself sent ye to my door for a nicht's hospitality?"

"He sent me in your general direction, for which I'll ever be most grateful. But hold on, Fiona. Are you saying what's just been going on here was because of the MacMillan chief?"

"Of course. Did ye think I was a wayward wench who slept wi' strangers wandering in off the street?"

"Heaven forbid! But hold on, honey lamb. You told me when I asked that you weren't no member of that MacMillan clan."

"I'm not. Clan Duffy is but allied wi' the MacMillans in peace and war. Didna ye ken that, darling Custis?"

He repressed a groan and settled for a quietly spoken, "I do now." But he wasn't very pleased. For here he was in bed with a woman of one warring faction before he'd even had one word with the other side!

The newspaperman, Redford, had warned him that these Scotch folk took it serious if one even drank in the same saloon as their enemies. Now he'd just wound up in bed with a gal Clan Campbell had to have down on their hate list.

Meanwhile, she was moving under him, pulsing her internal muscles on his semi-erection. So it didn't stay semi— and, what the hell, the fat was in the fire, and as long as *he* was in *her* . . .

It was even nicer the second time, now that they'd gotten one another's rhythm down pat. Again she came ahead of him. So he rolled her over on her tummy and mounted her from the rear, to finish wild in another way. It drove Fiona

47

even wilder. She was chewing the bottom sheet and beating on the mattress with her fists as she arched her spine to take it all while she contracted in orgasm on his thrusting shaft. He returned the compliment by coming so hard he could feel it all the way down to his toes.

As he collapsed atop her, she sighed. "That was bonny indeed. As long as ye're up there, can ye see if that beacon is yet burning, dear?"

He straightened up, still in her, and glanced out the window next to the bed. "It sure is," he said. "Matter of fact, it looks like a burning cross of some kind. You folks don't have the KKK in these parts, do you?"

She sighed and said, "Och, if only it *was* those daft Yankee copycats who call themselves the Ku Klux Klan. But that's no schoolboy prank meant to frighten darkies, Custis. It's the real auld Rood of Fire and Sword!"

They were in an awkward position for conversation, and this was getting interesting. So Longarm withdrew from her, found his shirt on the floor, where he'd figured it might have wound up, and fished out a smoke and a light before sitting beside her on the bed. "Let's share us a smoke and get our second wind while you tell me what in the hell is going on out there," he suggested.

As he struck a light and puffed the cheroot into action, Fiona propped herself up on the pillows against the headboard, looking mighty nice in the kindly light of the waterproof match. "Everyone knows of the auld Highland war beacons, darling," she said. "Your silly American Klan stole the idea from us."

"You burn crosses in front of colored folks' houses in Scotland?"

"Dinna talk daft. We Gaidheals are a sober race. The auld burning roods were never meant to frighten anyone. They were a signal for the clan warriors to gather. Ye might say it's a time-tested signal for the declaring of war to the death."

Longarm looked out the window again and said, "From

48

here it looks like that cross is burning on some rise in Campbell territory, and the last I saw of the chief Mac-Millan, he was drunk as a skunk."

"Aye, our Toshach does have a taste for the creature. But have no fear he'll not be able to defend himself, drunk or sober. Ye'll be safe enough here wi' me, darling, for I'm a woman and ye're no MacMillan."

Longarm studied on getting up and strapping on his gun as he puffed on his smoke. But he could see that had to be a mighty dumb move. At least one MacMillan or three weren't all that fond of him, and he didn't know a single Campbell. He doubted he wanted to meet one for the first time coming out of a MacMillan woman's house, either.

He offered Fiona a drag on the smoke. "Well, I can't say I ain't forted up in mighty pleasant surroundings," he remarked. "But you said before that something was odd about that war signal, Fiona. How odd? I'm trying to learn fast, but this clan business is more complicated than I expected it to be."

She handed him back the cheroot and sighed. "It's like learning the pipes. Ye have to grow up wi' them, I fear. Ainly the sennachies ken a' the clan traditions. As ye see, I'm ainly a wee woman."

He took a drag on the smoke with one hand on her perky breast as he said, "A damn pretty woman, too. But don't be so modest. You talk the lingo and you said you noticed something funny about that burning cross. So let me in on it, damn it. Do I have to torture it out of you?"

She laughed, placing a hand on the back of his to press it closer to her heart as she explained. "Ye've no need to torture me, darling. Though I've some punishment left for *ye* between my thighs before this nicht is over. I only thought it odd that the signal was not where I would ha' expected the Campbells to burn it. There's a grand prairie rise closer to the Double C. Yet they've lit the rood on open range out of sight from Duncan Campbell's windows there. But, och, what do *I* ken aboot the ways of warring men? It's certain

49

no MacMillan lit the cross. For, convenient or not, it's burning on Campbell range!"

He started to wonder why he was fooling with a cheroot when Fiona felt so much nicer. He could tell from the way her hand had crept into his lap that she was rested, too. But he took another determined puff. "Hold on, gal. It's early yet, and I know what my next move around *you* ought to be!"

She was holding on indeed as he added, insistently, "The funny habits and outlandish ways of you Scots Wells folk has me half licked before I can even ask sensible questions. Do you have a book with all them odd notions writ in plain old American, Fiona?"

"The clan histories are an oral record, kept by the auld Sennacies. You Sassenach would call them story tellers, I suppose. I've heard some Lowlander named Logan once wrote a history of the Highland clans. My late father said the poor loon had half of it wrong. But Logan wrote in English. I've no idea where a copy could be foond."

"Is there a library in town that might have it, Fiona?"

"A library in Scots Wells? Och, we dinna even ha' a decent dress shop! But what are ye looking to discover, Custis?"

"Someone's declared war and I'm in over my head, total, on this Scotch feud business. I've learned more than I ever thought I'd want to know since riding in this evening, but it's still mighty confusing. For instance, I figured a clan was a clan and that was that. Now you tell me you MacPhees is riding with MacMillan, even though you belong to another clan entire. Explain *that*, at least, and I'll put out this fool smoke."

She laughed and said, "I'll hold you to that promise," and held on to him, too, as she went on. "It's simple enough to a Highlander. Since the Massacre of Glencoe, almost every clan of the West Highlands has been against the treacherous Campbells. The sennachies say that once when

50

the Cameron of Lochiel was met on the field of battle wi' Clan Chatten..."

"Hold it," he cut in. "Can't we get more up to date, honey lamb?"

She stroked his erection teasingly as she said, "It was not my idea to talk of auld clan feuds. But if ye want to understand us, ye ha' to ken that we Celts have long memories."

"That's for damned sure! Was this other fight before or after this Massacre everyone keeps jawing about?"

"After, of course. As I was saying, Cameron and Chatten was ready to have a battle in the Glen Mhor when word came that the Campbell of Argyle was marching through the braes of Inverness, searching for men wha'd stolen some of his bonny cows, I believe. His reason doesna matter. The point is that on learning the hated Campbells were coming, the two enemy Toshachs dropped what they were doing and joined forces to drive the False Argyle back to his own side of the mountains. See?"

"I'm starting to. All right, I know I'll be sorry I asked, but what's this Massacre business all you other clans are so het up about?"

She must have taken the old tale seriously, for she took her hand off his groin as she spoke in a deadly serious tone. "That's a shame Clan Campbell wi' never live doon! It was during the rising of the Jacobite clans in the 1690s..."

"Oh, God, what's a *Jacobite?*"

"Clans loyal to the hoose of Stuart and the true Kings of Alban, of course. Campbell, as usual, chose to fight on the winning English side. The rising was put doon. Peace was declared. The fighting was over. Or at least it was supposed to be. So when the Campbell of Glenlyon marched into Glencoe wi' a regiment of government troops along wi' his dirty Campbells, MacIan MacDonald offered no resistance and made them welcome, as was the custom in the Highlands in times of peace."

"Peace must have been a mighty rare condition. What happened next?"

"Och, what would one expect, from Clan Campbell? Glenlyon *accepted* the hospitality of MacIan MacDonald and his people. Sae they all sat doon to *break bread* together. Have ye any idea of the sacred trust involved in sooch an act?"

"Sure. Everybody knows you don't act ornery once you've broke bread with a gent. Is that when the massacre started?"

"Heavens, no. MacIan wasn't *that* trusting a mon, and remember, he was entertaining *Campbells!* No, what happened was that the treacherous Glenlyon and his soldiers stayed under the thatch of the MacDonald as guests for many a day and nicht, drinking toasts to their host and the new-found peace, until one nicht, when the MacDonalds were a' fast asleep, Glenlyon gave the signal. In the slaughter that followed, everyone but a few quick-witted survivors perished by the sword or gun, most in their own beds."

Longarm whistled softly and said, "That was mighty raw. For *I* can grasp what a dirty trick it was, and I'm not even Scotch."

Then he snuffed out the cheroot and said, "Speaking of raw and speaking of grasping, let's make it come right!"

So they went crazy together for a while and he forgot the old clan grudges while they tried every position that didn't hurt. He didn't know what the rules of Scotch loving might be, so he let her show him. And it was surprising how French habits seemed to have gotten all the way to the Highlands.

But later, as she fell asleep with her head on his shoulder, Longarm was still wide awake and wishing she was, too. He didn't want to lay her any more. His muscles couldn't have taken it even had he been up to it. But he sure had a lot of questions to ask. He finally gave up and decided to worry about them come morning. The distant burning cross had now gone out. He'd likely find out soon enough if that cross meant anything important.

Chapter 5

Next morning, after he'd had Fiona and breakfast, Longarm left by way of the back door to mosey into town. He doubted old Fiona would run out onto her front porch to announce to one and all he'd spent the night with her, and Petunia was out of sight in the stable, so he figured their friendship could be kept secret.

Longarm and his gracious hostess hadn't been the only folk in town to notice the burning cross the night before, of course. Everyone he passed seemed to be talking about it. At least, they did until they noticed a strange face. Then they stopped as if someone had clamped a hand over their mouths.

Walking down the MacMillan side of the street didn't tell Longarm anything new. So when he got opposite the Argyle Arms, the saloon the Campbells were said to drink in, Longarm walked across and parted the batwing doors.

A piano had been playing inside as he approached. It stopped as if someone had poleaxed the professor when the boys inside saw Longarm in the doorway. There were a mess of townspeople and boys dressed cow bellied up to the bar. He doubted they'd all been drinking that silently a few seconds ago. He kept his face dumb and his gun hand polite as he found a vacant space near the end of the bar. The space got even more vacant as the boys edged away. Longarm smiled at the bartender.

The bartender said, "We don't serve Sassenachs in here."

Longarm went on smiling as he replied. "That's all right, friend. I don't drink Sassenachs anyway. I'll have a draft beer."

Someone in the crowd laughed, or snickered at least, but the bartender didn't look amused. He shook his head and said, "Do yourself a favor and get out while you still can, stranger. They say Gordie Thompson's riding in from the Double C, and they burned the cross last night."

"I noticed," Longarm said. "I'm glad old Gordie is on his way in. It saves me having to go looking for him."

A timid-looking man murmured, "Oh, Jesus!" and headed for the door. But a cowhand stopped him, saying, "Stand and be counted, Andrew MacIvor. Any man who doesn't stand by his clan when the rood's been lit is a man who'd eat shit for breakfast in bed with his mother."

There was a growl of agreement.

Little MacIvor whined, "Jesus, I'm a grocer!" But he moved back to stand against the wall, licking his lips and trying not to piss his britches. Longarm could see MacIvor was as scared of his own faction as he was of the other. It wasn't Longarm's problem. Longarm's problem was headed his way, clanking lots of spurs and swishing batwing chaps. The cowhand's mouth was noisy, too, as he stopped at gunfighting range from Longarm and asked, in a bull-like bellow, "Who in the hell are you, a hired gun sent by the MacMillans?"

Longarm shook his head and said, "Nope. They make me dress like a tinhorn since President Hayes took office. They say he eats supper in a boiled shirt as well. I'm a U.S. federal deputy. I'm called Longarm, just in case you heard of my rep out in these parts. If *you* are looking to get a rep, I'd best advise you that there's more like me where I come from."

"I don't care who you are or how many more there are at home like you, little darling. You just mentioned the name of Gordie Thompson in a tone that implies you don't know *his* rep! You want to tell us what business you have with Gordie before he gets here? Gordie don't listen too good."

"I'll tell him when he shows up, friend," Longarm said. "Do you have a name, or are folks supposed to just run when they see you coming?"

The big tough laughed and roared out, "What do you know? The rascal ain't heard of Ian Mhor MacDermid, neither!"

"Well, fair is fair, since you don't seem scared of me," Longarm said. "I'd buy you a drink, Ian Mhor, if I could convince this fool bartender how thirsty I am."

"Give us two shots of Glenspey, here, damn it!" Ian Mhor roared.

Before Longarm could make the gesture, the big cowhand added, "I'm paying. It wouldn't be right to gutshoot a man who's just bought me a drink."

As the bartender slid a bottle and two shotglasses across the mahogany and moved back out of the way, Longarm said, "That sounds fair. I won't gutshoot you, neither, pard."

MacDermid laughed incredulously and replied, "You won't shoot me at all, little darling. I hardly ever let folks shoot me. It's generally the other way around."

Longarm didn't answer. He turned from Ian Mhor to reach for the bottle as someone in the crowd murmured, "Oh-oh!"

But nothing happened. Longarm hadn't expected it to.

55

He'd faced many a gunslick in his day. Some of them even made as much noise working up to a fight as old Ian Mhor. But Longarm knew this type. He blustered too hard for a man facing an outnumbered and outgunned stranger in his own saloon. Longarm poured two drinks, giving the bully all the rope he wanted to take. Then, when he saw that nothing was going to happen, he turned back to the glowering hulk and slid a drink his way. "Here's mud in your eye, pard," he said.

"You was watching me in that mirror, wasn't you?"

Longarm lifted his own drink with a carefree smile. "I see you really are an old gunslick. A man would have to get up mighty early to pull the wool over your eyes, right?"

"Right," said Ian Mhor, mollified by the tribute to his legendary prowess. Had he been known as far away as Rabbit Wash, Longarm would have heard of him, but the deputy didn't mind flattering the fool.

The saloon-rail bully swallowed his drink, reached for the bottle near Longarm's elbow, and poured another. "You were going to tell me what you wanted with Gordie, remember?" he said.

Longarm said, "I never gossip behind a man's back. I'll tell Thompson what I want with him when I see him."

Ian Mhor's eyes blazed dangerously. Then he noticed the way Longarm's eyes met his and, not liking what he saw, shrugged. "Well, it's your funeral. They burned the cross last night, and Gordie's on the prod."

Longarm downed his own malt liquor and poured another. "I said I'd noticed. You don't talk Scotch—Scottish, or whatever. But from your name you must know more than me about such matters. How come your ramrod's all hot and bothered about the cross his own clan burned? I should think he'd have woke up feeling proud and chipper."

MacDermid started to say something, but a more sensible voice from somewhere in the crowd called out, "Whist, MacDermid. The mon's the law as well as a stranger!"

Longarm couldn't tell who had spoken, but the voice

had sounded Scotch. There were a couple of old goats in the saloon who were likely, but he decided not to press it. The gent had just said not to talk to the law, and wasn't likely to do so himself.

As Longarm studied the fool situation he'd walked into, and before anyone else in the Argyle Arms could make it tenser, a voice from outside started yelling something awful. The bartender had the best view out the window at the end of the bar. He gasped and shouted, "Oh, God, it's the MacMillan in the flesh, with a dozen riders backing his play!"

The familiar voice switched to English, calling out, "We ken ye're in there, Gordie Thompson! Come out and face us like a mon, ye windbag burner of wee stickies in the nicht!"

The meek little grocer dropped to his hands and knees and crawled under a table.

The bartender said, "You'd better speak for us, Ian Mhor. I fear the MacMillan is filled with the creature, and if someone doesn't go out, he'll be coming in. Go tell him Gordie's not here, for God's sake!"

But Ian Mhor was headed for the back, apparently heeding a sudden call of nature.

"What about you, Tavish Burnes?" someone asked, but was answered with, "Don't talk daft. I'm a blacksmith, not a gunfighter, and there's a dozen MacMillans out there!"

Longarm put down his shotglass. "Don't get your bowels in an uproar, boys. I'll go see what they want," he said.

As he headed for the doorway, someone said, "You'll be shot down like a dog the moment you show your face, you fool!"

Longarm thought the warning was right neighborly considering how they'd been rawhiding him up to now, but he didn't answer. He had more important chores.

"Hold your fire, MacMillan," he called out. "I ain't Gordie Thompson, but I'm coming out anyway."

Then he stepped outside, feeling mighty like a bullseye,

but a man toting a badge for a living couldn't act like a sissy.

A shot rang out and the saloon window to Longarm's right dissolved in a cloud of shattered glass. But Longarm managed with some effort not to flinch or crawfish. He knew anybody missing so wide with a rifle gun had to be just funning. As he stepped into the dusty street he heard old Calum MacMillan shouting, "Stop that, ye fool! Canna ye see it's that law mon I told ye aboot?"

Longarm knew it was going to be all right for now. He headed over to where the old Toshach and a mess of younger gents were covering the saloon and everything between from the cover of the watering troughs and such on the MacMillan side of the street.

As he stepped up to join them, old Calum frowned at Longarm and demanded, "What was a decent Christian doing in the Argyle Arms this morning, Deputy Long?"

Before Longarm could answer, another shot rang out, this time from behind him. As it showered him and the old Toshach with water meant for horses, MacMillan grabbed Longarm by the right sleeve and hauled him bodily through a glassed shop door without bothering to open it, crying out, "Och, is there no end to the treachery of the breed!"

Longarm pulled free, brushed broken glass from his tweed coat as he growled, "Never grab a man by his gun arm, damn it!"

He would have said more, but his words were drowned out by the roar of gunfire all around. The MacMillans were firing into the Argyle Arms from cover all up and down their side of the street. The Campbells were firing back, of course, so Longarm shoved the old man to the floor as a slug parted the air where they'd just been standing.

Old Calum had his own Patterson Conversion out and was crawling for the doorway, cursing in Gaelic. Longarm sat up, grabbed him by both booted ankles, and hauled him back as another bullet tore a long sliver from the threshold the old fool would have had his chest across if more sensible gents weren't about.

MacMillan growled, "Let go of my shins, ye loon! It's war they want and it's war they'll have!"

"Simmer down, god damn it! They didn't fire first. *Your* boys did!"

"Not true! Not true! It was at your own back they fired, ye wee daft fool!" MacMillan spluttered.

"I noticed," Longarm said calmly. "Can't you get your boys to stop? That rifle ball taking out the saloon window was never fired by anyone named Campbell. As to the one meant for you and me, who's to say where it come from? Did you see who pegged a shot into that watering trough?"

"Nae, but it came from the Campbell side of yon street!"

Longarm had made the mistake of relaxing his grip as they spoke. The old man suddenly kicked free and before Longarm could stop him, Calum MacMillan leaped up and ran out the door, shouting, "It's nae use, Clan Campbell! Prepare to meet yer doom!"

Then he came right back in, blood running down the side of his face from under the fancy hat, to fall full length on the floor as yet another bullet whizzed over him at waist level.

Longarm reached out to drag the old man to cover by the heels again. Crouching over the dead or unconscious chief, Longarm peeled off the blood-sticky Stetson and whistled.

The silver clan badge and the mighty thick skull Longarm had figured had conspired to save such brains as the old coot had. The soft-nosed pistol slug was buried in the ruined disc of thick silver. But MacMillan was going to wake up with a walloping headache, if he ever woke up at all.

The side of his scalp was split and bleeding heavily, but without the pulsing spurts that showed a cut artery. The old man's head was already swelling like he'd been sat on by a mighty big bee. That was another good sign. If the skull had cracked, the swelling would be working in instead of out.

Longarm left him be for now and moved to the shattered window of the shop. He raised his head cautiously and called out, "Angus Bethune, you silly bastard, where are you at?"

A gruff voice called back, "Here! What do you want, Sassenach?"

Longarm shouted, "Cease fire and get your ass in here, boy! Your chief is hurt and he needs help pronto!"

From across the street a voice Longarm recognized as that of the bully, Ian Mhor, shouted out, "Did you hear that, boys? I nailed their Toshach!"

Longarm pegged a round through the window at the Argyle Arms, aiming high so he wouldn't hurt anybody, while he kept them from getting any silly thoughts about charging.

Angus Bethune crawled around the doorjamb, spitting splinters and cursing like a muleskinner. He saw MacMillan stretched out near Longarm and gasped. "Oh, Jesus, is he dead?" he cried.

Longarm started to say it looked like simple concussion, but that would have been dumb. So he said, instead, "No, but he will be soon if you don't get him to a doctor. If I cover you from here could you haul him out the back door and carry him to some MacMillan sawbones?"

Angus said, "I could, but it's my duty to stand and fight like a man for my clan."

"Have you got wax in your ears, old son? Your clan chief may die if he don't get medical attention, and then where will you be? Oh, I see. If you let your chief die, you'll run for the job, right?"

"You lying Sassenach son of a bitch!" Angus Bethune gasped. "I'll remember those filthy words from a stranger's lips!" He bent to grab the wounded man under the armpits and start hauling him toward the back of the store.

Longarm waited until Bethune had kicked out the back door and was out of the fight for now. With their chief and big hoorah gone, the other MacMillans might listen to the sweet voice of reason. "Cease firing, MacMillans!" Longarm shouted. "I aim to have a parley with the Campbells!"

If anybody heard him above the roar of their own guns, they didn't pay any attention. Longarm swore at both sides as he crouched in the shot-out window, trying to figure out what to do next.

A posse of two dozen riders came down the street riding hell for leather in a cloud of dust and gunsmoke. It looked impressive as hell, but it was mighty poor cavalry tactics.

Someone shouted, "It's Gordie Thompson for Clan Campbell!"

Longarm winced and waited for saddles to proceed to empty. Gordie Thompson, if that was him riding tall beyond reason on a big dapple gray, rode his men from the Double C right into the crossfire of the opposing factions.

But as they reined in, blurry in the dry fog now filling the street, the shooting closer to Longarm whimpered away and he heard boot heels pounding on floorboards as back doors busted open.

Longarm took out his wallet, removed his badge, and pinned it to his breast. *Did you ever get the feeling you was all alone in the house, old son?* he thought.

He stood up, holstered his .44 after reloading it, and stepped out of the gaping doorway. Nobody noticed him at first in the haze and confusion. Then, as he started across the street, Ian Mhor shouted, "That's him, Gordie! That's the Sassenach who was gunning for you!"

Two giants strode to meet Longarm in the haze. The dismounted Gordie Thompson was a head taller than Ian Mhor, which was ridiculous to begin with. As they came closer Longarm said, pleasant-voiced, "I knowed a couple of brothers named Thompson one time, down Dodge City way. You must be kin. They was big and mean-looking, too."

Closer in, Gordie Thompson was better looking and perhaps a shade brighter than Ian Mhor, which wasn't saying much. His voice was soft-spoken but deep as the growl of a bear down a well. "I hear you've been taking my name in vain, friend," he said to Longarm.

"I've been looking to meet up with you. Before you make any silly moves I'll remind you I'm wearing a U. S. federal badge."

"We live by a higher law here, Sassenach. It's the custom of our people to settle matters among themselves!"

"Yeah, I'll keep it in mind. But you sound mighty American to be carrying on so foreign-natured. Can we do some drinking while we talk? My mouth is full of 'dobe dust and gunsmoke. How about you?"

Thompson scowled and growled, "Ian Mhor was right. You're some kind of lunatic. Stand aside and let me get at them MacMillans, you fool! I'll deal with you later, after I take care of *important* enemies!"

But Longarm held his ground. "Simmer down," he said. "The fight's over for now. The other side run off when they seen you coming. They must scare easy. I'd say you Campbells won this round. For one of you shot old man MacMillan by accident. If he dies, it means a murder warrant, sure as hell, unless a neutral observer like yours truly testifies he went down with a considerable gun in his hand. I'm trying to be a friend to all concerned here, Gordie."

"I need no friends. I ride with a big clan. So get the hell outten my way or I'm coming through you!" Thompson said.

Longarm didn't move. Thompson slapped leather.

Then he froze, his long-barreled Peacemaker still hung up in its tie-down, as he morosely contemplated the muzzle of Longarm's .44 almost sticking up his nose.

Longarm snapped, "Ian Mhor! You back off sudden and back off with your hands *polite,* unless you want to be spattered with this fool's brains before I blow your belt buckle out your asshole!"

Ian Mhor was a good listener. Longarm had figured he might be.

When they were alone in the haze, Gordie Thompson slowly slid his own gun back in its holster, let go of it, and said, "All right, you're faster than possible. What happens now?"

Longarm put his own gun away. "We have a drink and a talk. I aim to drink beer, but you can pick the saloon."

Thompson said, "I don't want to drink with you."

Longarm sighed. "This surely is one unfriendly town. All right, I'll make it short and sweet, since anyone can see you don't have much worth interest in your thick skull. I've spoken about this dumb feud with the chief of the Mac-Millans. Now I aim to hear your side of the story from the Campbell chief. That'd be Duncan Campbell of the Double C spread, right?"

"It would. But how do you expect to get to him alive?"

"I was hoping to ride in friendly, with your invite. What's the matter? Have you got your chief locked in the storm cellar while you give orders in his name?"

"That's a goddamned lie! Nobody but Duncan the Grim gives orders to Clan Campbell, and one of his orders is that he doesn't want to be disturbed as he plans the ruination of his enemies out at the ranch."

"But you could ride me through his defense pickets, couldn't you?"

Thompson shook his head. "I could, but I won't, even if you wave that sneaky gun at me some more! You don't understand us at all, stranger. Duncan the Grim gave *orders!*"

"Oh, shit," Longarm said, "if anybody hereabouts understands what's going on, he has to be a lunatic. All right, I'll get to your chief some other damned way, in my own good time. Meanwhile, can you talk to me about that cross you boys burned on the rise last night?"

Gordie Thompson looked sincerely puzzled. "I don't know who done that. It wasn't me. It was hearing of it as brought me to town. My Toshach ordered me to find out what was going on."

"Hold it right there! Are you saying not even the chief of the Campbells knows who burned a cross on Campbell range? I thought a burning cross was a declaration of war."

Thompson nodded grimly. "It is. Everyone knows that. Why did you think we rode in shooting?"

Longarm considered. "All right," he said finally. "What you'd best do now is ride back out, not shooting, before the MacMillans regroup under Angus Bethune, or, even worse, old Calum wakes up with a splitting headache. Somebody's trying to make trouble for both sides here. Even I can see that, and butterscotch sticks to the roof of my mouth!"

Thompson said, "I know the ways of the Highlands, and it's plain some MacMillan set a rood aflame on our own range as a taunt and a dare!"

"Mayhaps. Is that the usual custom at such times?" Longarm asked.

He saw by the flicker of consideration in the taller man's oyster-gray eyes that Gordie Thompson was at least a little bit brighter than he looked. "As a matter of fact, it's not," he said thoughtfully. "But the killing of MacTavish was a sneaky fairy trick, too. It's well known the Children of the Mist don't fight like real men!"

"Oh, shit! All right, I give up. Who in thunder are the Children of the Mist?" Longarm asked impatiently.

"Outlaws. Men of broken clans who haunt the glens with no duthas to call their own, and no regard for the laws of God or man."

"You mean like old Rob Roy in a book I read once?"

"Oh, *he* followed *some* rules. His mother was a Campbell, after all. But some MacGregors were known for treachery beyond the bounds of decency, and the MacMillans were always Jacobite Malignants, so . . ."

"Stop right there. Since you know so much, were any MacMillans mixed up in this Childish Mist business?"

Grudgingly, Thompson conceded, "They were a landed clan with claims recorded by the Lord Lyon, before the '45, of course. But who's to say what they've sunk to since then? Sheriff MacTavish was stabbed in the back with no declaration of feud!"

"So I heard. And your chief is sitting on the murder weapon, which I aim to have a look at while I hear his side. You could save us both a lot of needless fuss if you'd ride me out there, Gordie."

Thompson shook his head and started to say something. But Longarm sighed and said, "I know. Orders. It's been nice jawing with you, old son, but I reckon I'd best go get my mount and do some riding."

He turned away. The haze was starting to settle by now. As he headed back for Fiona's, Thompson called after him, "You'll never get within a mile of the main house! Duncan the Grim gave orders!"

Longarm stepped up on the walk and stomped his boots as he dusted himself off with his Stetson. *He thinks that's your only problem, old son?* he asked himself. *It's Monday morning and by now Billy Vail is at the office and staring pensive at his banjo clock! These fool Scotchmen ain't seen mad, till they've seen Billy Vail in a surly mood!*

Chapter 6

As Longarm rode Petunia out of Scots Wells, he intended at first to visit the Double C, whether Duncan the Grim wanted visitors or not. But as he considered the odds, his conscience bothered him a mite. He knew it was only right that he should give the office at least a hint that he was up here in Custer County instead of dead drunk in some alley in Denver. Sending a wire could be difficult if he wound up dead and buried on the lone prairie. His superiors would never know what had happened to him—and, worse yet, his replacements would be riding blind into this ridiculous situation.

On the other hand, once he confessed jumping the gun and sneaking up here solo, Billy Vail was bound to load Smiley and Dutch aboard the next northbound Burlington. Longarm needed a couple of other deputies like he needed a busted saddle girth. Smiley and Dutch were tolerable in a fight, but he had enough worries on his plate, and riding herd on them would only slow him down.

He heeled Petunia to the top of a rise to look around at the horizon line. Nobody seemed to be trailing them this morning. "Well, Petunia, we'd best just ride into Rabbit Wash and make use of the Western Union there," he said. "With luck, them pesky deputies won't make it here until late in the afternoon. And, what the hell, it's still early. With even more luck, they won't catch up with us for a spell. Fiona asked us not to tell anyone how hospitable she is."

Having made up his mind, Longarm made up for wasted time by loping Petunia along the ridges, avoiding the wagon trace and the wash entirely, now that he knew his way about up here.

He rode into Rabbit Wash without hearing even a distant gunshot. Rabbit Wash looked even less interesting in mid-morning. He reined in before a saloon and tethered Petunia. As he stepped up onto the walk he saw that the saloon wasn't open yet. A little old gal in a sunbonnet was coming down the walk. He tipped his hat and asked her if she knew where the telegraph office was. She blushed like a rose and told him it was up the street a few doors. Then she ran off, as if to save her virtue. He chuckled and muttered, "Not hardly, little darling. I like my she-males at least halfway pretty."

He passed the newspaper office, paying it little mind, and found his way to the Western Union. He went in, picked up a stub of a pencil and a telegraph form, and proceeded to explain his whereabouts and recent actions. Considering how little he thought he knew, he was surprised that it took two whole pages just to list his suspects and suspicions, keeping things short and sweet.

He called the clerk over and said, "As you can see, this is a mighty long message. I'm sending her collect to the Denver U. S. Marshal's office. But it seems a shame to cause the taxpayers of these United States needless expense. So we'd best send it as a night letter."

The clerk glanced at the clock on the wall and said, "It won't get there before about this time Tuesday morning if you send it night letter, sir."

Longarm grinned like a coyote peering through a hole in the fence. "I know. You just do the best you can with my night letter, hear?"

The clerk said they'd get around to sending it sometime around midnight, when the wires were slow and cheaper. Longarm told him there was no hurry, thanked him, and went back out, feeling pleased with himself. He'd done his duty, damn it. He'd left a mite early and wired as soon as he could. What did Billy Vail want, egg in his beer? It wasn't anyone's fault that there wasn't a telegraph office at the county seat. Anyone leaving Denver had a right to expect one.

As he strolled back to mount Petunia and rode out to more serious chores, he noticed the front door of the *Custer County Clarion* office was ajar. But when he glanced in, he saw nobody behind the counter inside. He shrugged and started to move on. Then he noticed that the brass spittoon by the counter had been kicked over, messy as hell. He frowned and eased the unlocked door open, listening instead of yelling.

There wasn't a sound coming from the back. If Nancy was back there helping with the printing, she and Silas Redford sure worked silent. He called out, "Anyone here?" and was answered by a muffled moan.

He drew his .44 and moved down the counter to open the gate. Then he reconsidered and vaulted the counter to land in a gunfight crouch on the far side.

He saw Nancy bound and gagged on the floor just a few feet away. Her eyes were as big as saucers as she met his gaze. He nodded good morning to her and whispered, "Nod your head if we're alone."

She did. So he holstered his gun and moved to kneel and

removed the gag from her mouth first. As he started to untie the rest of her, she gasped, "Oh, thank God you came! Mr. Redford left for Cheyenne just a few minutes ago and won't be back until late tonight. I thought I was going to have to spend the whole day here, and I have to...Never mind."

He got her untied and helped her to her feet. The dishwater blonde looked handsomer without her granny specs and with the severe bun on her head loosened up like that. He asked, "What happened? Who tied you up?"

But she darted past him to run around the press and slam a door behind her. The door was thin, so he didn't have to call out to ask what she was doing.

That reminded him that he hadn't taken a leak for a spell, either. But human beings had to act more polite about such matters than horses and other sensible critters. He lit a cheroot and waited. She came out, beet-red, and said, "I'm sorry. I've been tied up for quite a while."

"It's something even Queen Victoria must do, at least once a year, ma'am," he said. "To tell the truth, I was fixing to ask you about the sanitary facilities of this establishment. But now that I know I can save the shock to your delicate ears. Meanwhile, what happened here? Who tied you up?"

She shook her head and replied, "I don't know who they were. They were wearing kerchiefs over their faces and they were dressed like cowhands."

"That's not an outfit as attracts attention in these parts, ma'am. Now that the suspects have been described, sort of, what about their motive? Did they rob you of cash or—well—trifle with you personal?"

"They grabbed me and bound me hand and foot. Then they put a gag in my mouth and said they'd kill me if I let out one peep."

Longarm started to say that wasn't what he'd meant. But he knew womankind could be divided into them as reported a rape and them as would not. So he said, "Tell it any way you like, but tell it. What do you reckon they was after, Miss Nancy?"

She shrugged and said, "I don't have any idea. There isn't much money in the till and they never went near it, anyway. After they tied me up they went in the back and rummaged around. I thought at first they meant to destroy the galleys. We've been threatened about some of the news we print. But they'd have made more noise than I heard if they scattered type on the floor, so..."

"Let's take a look," Longarm said, moving toward the rear with her trailing. He got around the big flatbed press and saw the galleys of type and a composing table covered with some of the next edition set up, staring at the pressed-tin ceiling. He saw the open door of the water closet, too, so he said, "Excuse me a minute," and went inside to take advantage of the indoor plumbing.

She was standing by the composing table with her back to him when he rejoined her. The nape of her neck was the color of a pretty sunset.

He joined her at the table and regarded the set type. He asked when it figured to be published and she said, "It's the weekend edition. We only put out one paper a week."

"Yeah, filling up a daily could be a chore in this town. See where they might have messed up some type, ma'am?"

She shook her head. "No. It's locked in the frame and it hasn't been trifled with. I don't know exactly what all those columns say. Mr. Redford writes the news items in his head as he sets the type."

Longarm leaned forward, accidentally placing his hand against hers as he mused aloud. "I can read backwards. It's starting to look like at least one of your intruders could, too. They come to read the *Custer County Clarion* early, before it could hit the stands."

She didn't move her hand from his as he scanned the set type, moving his lips as he had to to read backwards. It wouldn't have been all that interesting if it had been easier to read. Some fool woman had just had a baby and a farmer wanted to sell his John Deere plow, cheap. The rest of the news explained why they only put the paper out once a week. There wasn't anything due to be published that wasn't mighty dull. Redford hadn't mentioned anyone named MacMillan or Campbell. There was a small item about the forthcoming November elections. As far as Longarm could see, Redford hadn't even taken sides in it.

He straightened up and, as Nancy didn't seem to object to holding hands with him, left his with hers as he said, "Your boss told me he was a cautious gent. I'd say your visitors wanted to make sure. But if they were worried about him printing something mean about them, Redford must have been in a position to do so. Do you have any notion what that might have been, Miss Nancy?"

She shook her head, letting yet another strand of blonde hair fall to soften the outline of her face. "I just work here part time," she explained. "You saw for yourself yesterday that he sends me out of the office when he has anything serious to talk about. Sometimes I think he thinks I'm a blabbermouth."

"Well, that's putting it a mite strong, Miss Nancy. Right now I wish he'd been more open with his hired help. For there's no way of knowing, until Redford gets back from Cheyenne, what those masked men were worried about. How late do you figure he might be?"

"I've no idea. When he left he just told me to lock up at noon if nobody came to place any advertisings. He said he'd see me Tuesday morning. So he'll have to come back some time this evening."

"That makes sense. Did he tell you why he was going to Cheyenne?" Longarm asked.

"He just said it was a business trip. Oh, I do know he took such money as we had in the till and put it in the bank down the street before he left town. That's how I knew those masked men weren't bent on robbery."

Longarm grinned down at her and said, "Bless your sweet hide, little gal, that's a pure clue! Hard cash is a temptation even to curious readers. So if they never bothered with the office till, they must have known it wasn't worth the bother."

She brightened. "Oh, they must have seen Mr. Redford go into the bank before he left town, then!" she exclaimed.

"That's what I figure. They watched him board the Cheyenne train—not wearing kerchiefs over their faces, I'd bet—and then they come here to read his paper in his absence. They were doubtless known here in town without their masks. Total strangers would have caused considerable talk in such a bitty wide spot in the road. I just come from the Western Union, where I identified myself as the law, and nobody saw fit to mention any suspicious characters across from the bank."

He took out his watch with the hand he didn't have next to hers. "Well, it's still early and your boss can't tell me what those rascals might have been worried about until he gets back from Cheyenne."

She sighed. "Oh, I thought mayhaps if we put our heads together and sort of studied on it while we held hands we could, you know..."

He started to say something about being in a hurry. But now she was holding his hand against her gut, and he could tell she didn't wear a corset.

"Well, I ain't in all that big a hurry," he said. "It'd be impolite to visit the Double C while they was setting down to noon dinner. Is there somewheres we could do the same, Miss Nancy? I had me a breakfast I figured would last me all day, but this prairie air seems to have revived my appetite."

She dimpled and said, "There's the tea shop down the walk, but it's awfully dear and the pastry is stale. Why don't we go to my place and let me rustle us up some sausage and eggs?"

He said that sounded even better, so she hung a closed sign in the door, got her specs from the drawer under the counter, and led him out the back way. He noticed she didn't put on the specs. She went on holding hands with him in public, too. He knew gals didn't often get to show off how pretty they might be in small towns. He wasn't sure he wanted to go on record as her intended. But it would be impolite to yank his hand away from a lady, and neither Fiona nor the widow woman in Denver was likely to be hanging clothes out to dry in Rabbit Wash as the local biddies exchanged gossip.

Nancy lived on the far side of the alley running behind the storefronts. Nobody seemed to pay them any mind as she led him in the back way. Her digs were on the top floor. She explained on the stairs that the folks who owned the house and lived downstairs were out of town right now. He wondered why she wanted him to know they were alone in the house. Then he told himself he sure was asking some dumb questions this morning.

Nancy's furnished and hired digs consisted of a closet, a tiny kitchen which had once been something else, and one fair-sized room mostly occupied by a fair-sized brass bedstead. She said another closet had been fitted with a flush commode, if he needed to go again. He said he didn't, so she sat him down on the bed beside her.

Longarm saw that she wasn't making any great effort to prepare sausage and eggs. He put his arm around her and reeled her in for a friendly kiss.

She kissed back, with considerable passion. But when they came up for air with his free hand on her breast she giggled and asked, "What about my home cooking you said you was so interested in, Deputy Long?"

He said, "Call me Custis. I know it's a dumb name, but I didn't pick it, and this ain't the time and place to talk formal. Your little stove out there is colder than a banker's heart. We can eat later, after we get around to warming it up. And, speaking of warming things up..."

They fell across the mattress together and he ran his hand over the interesting rolling prairie between her firm breasts and down to more serious regions. He began to inch up her skirts to get them out of the way. He'd already established that she wasn't wearing anything under them.

As he got to working on her she moaned in pleasure and

74

opened her thighs. But as he got two fingers in she rolled her mouth from his and gasped, "Oh, my God, what are you doing?"

He said, "Examining for evidence, honey. You said them rascals never trifled with you here. They sure must have been stupid."

She laughed and started moving her hips to meet his not-so-soothing massage. He could tell that she hadn't been raped, but she sure was willing to be screwed more gentle. So he let go of his advantage long enough to unbutton his fly. He just rolled into the saddle and shoved it where she must have expected, for she went crazy as hell on first contact.

He went a mite crazy, too. After making love that morning to a naked brunette, it felt quaint to lie with a blonde with her duds on. Nancy drew her bare legs up and locked her high-button shoes around his waist as they pounded their way to paradise. They came together, fast, like old friends. As he stopped moving, she smiled up at him with a dreamy expression in her nearsighted eyes and asked, "Do you always make love wearing a gunbelt and a ten-gallon hat, dear?"

He laughed and withdrew from her to start shucking right. "I've never worn a ten-gallon hat in my life. This is a plain old Colorado Crush—or it was."

She giggled and began to peel her own duds as he skimmed the Stetson across the room to land wherever it had a mind to. Starting with her advantage of only having a dress, knee-high stockings, and those shoes, Nancy beat him to the buff. As he was down to pants and boots she rolled across the bed to haul a pillow from under the coverlet, place it under her rump, and lean back in a mighty sassy position. "Hurry! I'm still hot as anything!" she pleaded.

That made two of them. Starting over with their clothes off felt like starting fresh with somebody new. The angle of attack was different, too, thanks to that firm pillow under her bounding derriere. She was slimmer built than Fiona and way shorter as well as twenty pounds lighter than the widow woman back home. But she sure could take all a man had to offer and then some. She was built tight, but surprisingly deep, as he discovered when she raised her ankles to lock them fondly around the nape of his neck. He started moving to suit the invitation. She reached down to fondle his balls as they bounced against her behind. It felt more uncomfortable than loving. So he stopped kissing her long enough to protest, "Easy with them treasures, little darling. Why are you mashing them so?"

"I want them inside me, too!" she moaned, suiting actions to her words as she damned near ruined him for life.

He said, "It won't work. Take the word of a man who's tried. I don't want to brag, but in case you hadn't noticed, I'm filling you mighty tight with what's already in there!"

She started to say something, groaned, and went limp under him, her head rolling from side to side as he kept pounding. She gasped, "Stop! You're driving me crazy!" But by the time he came again she was moving in a way that belied her protests. He stopped anyway. A man had to catch his breath now and again.

Nancy crooned, "Oh, that was wonderful. Are you still hot? Do you still think I'm pretty?"

"Honey, if you was any prettier Ellen Terry and the Jersey Lily would both commit suicide."

"You don't think I'm—well—forward?"

"I love it forwards, backwards, or sideways. I hope we're not fixing to have a tedious discussion of small-town morals, sweetheart. I'll say right out I've never gone along with Queen Victoria or even Lemonade Lucy Hayes in the White House when it comes to natural feelings."

"Yes, but you're a man. Everyone knows men are allowed to sow their wild oats, darling Custis."

"That may well be. But who in thunder would us horny rascals sow our wild oats with if nice gals like you didn't help out? I'm sure my pony loves me, but I'd sure look stupid doing this to old Petunia."

She laughed at the picture, then asked, "You don't consider me a naughty girl, then?"

"Hell, yes, you're naughty, bless your sweet rollicking rump! Naughty gals are my favorites. I hardly ever go to bed with prim and proper gals. Matter of fact, you'd be surprised how many prim and proper gals ain't when you get to know them."

She kissed him warmly and said, "You're just horrid, and I'm so glad. Let me get on top. I want to try something new."

That suited him. He was a mite winded, likely from the long ride to town. He withdrew and rolled on his back. She looked mighty sassy in the sunlight through her lace curtains as she forked a pale thigh across him and positioned herself above his semi-erection. She reached down between them and guided him in.

Nancy bounced and jerked for a spell, then she settled back down, engulfing him in hot pulsations that felt even tighter than before. It drove her insane, judging from the way she was bouncing. She cranked her legs around one at a time and placed a bare heel in each of his armpits. Then she leaned back, bracing herself with her hands on his knees, and gasped.

He knew he was coming, too, and they exploded together.

She fell over backwards, falling off his now-soft shaft with a sigh of contentment. He sighed too, and got up to head for the bathroom.

Nancy rolled over on her side with her eyes closed and said, "You know where the bathroom is. Please bring me a moist washcloth on the way back."

He said he would and rolled his legs off the bed to stand up, sort of stiff, and walk across the thick rug barefoot. As he passed the chair by the bed, he took his .44 along without thinking.

In her tiny water closet he wondered why. He wondered where the sink was, too. Then he remembered that the sink

77

was in the kitchen. It was likely the only one in the place. He saw the washcloth and towel hanging on the wall, though. He tucked the .44 under an arm and bent over to wet the rag in the toilet bowl. What the hell, the water was clean, between flushings.

He cleaned himself off and wrung the rag out fresh for Nancy. Then he ran the towel through his crotch. The damned fool gun was awkward, but he managed. He hung the towel up, draped the damp rag over the muzzle of his .44, and opened the door again.

As he did so, the closet door facing him flew open and the black-clad total stranger who'd been hiding in it all this time raised the .45 in his left hand with a knowing sneer!

His expression turned to one of pained concern as Longarm fired the .44 under the washcloth at what was point-blank range for both of them. The left-handed gunman slammed against the wall behind him and slid down it, glassy-eyed and slack-jawed, as somewhere a woman was screaming.

Longarm kicked the stranger's gun clear of the remains, just in case, and moved to shut Nancy up, soothing, "Hush your face, damn it! Don't you reckon we ought to get some clothes on before the law arrives?"

The blonde was staring wide-eyed past Longarm at the legs poking out of her closet. She gasped, "My God, you killed him!"

Longarm said, "I noticed. Snap out of it, girl! The sound of a gunshot tends to draw attetnion, and the town law will be pounding on doors up and down the block any minute. Who was that silly son of a bitch, anyway?"

"I don't know. I never saw him before. Would I have let you screw me if I knew another man was up here?"

Longarm sat on the bed beside her and started to at least get himself dressed decent as she got up, naked, to go and have a better look at the cadaver. She came back shaking her head and saying, "It wasn't one of the men who tied me up. His clothes are different. Oh, Custis, what are we going to do?"

"First you start getting dressed while I explain. Number one, I am the law, so it's only natural for me to shoot burglars. I do it all the time. As I recall, I found you tied up at the *Clarion.* I naturally escorted you home. You were worried about the folks downstairs not being home. So I naturally said I'd go ahead up and make sure your digs was safe. That's when this jasper popped out at me with a gun in his hand and—yeah, I like it. Is it all coming back to you now, honey?"

She was still sobbing and fussing as he got her dressed decent and led her downstairs to look up the local law. She said she was a poor fibber and that he'd have to do most of the talking. He said, "I will. Remember, you didn't see much. You was waiting on the stairs when I surprised the prowling bastard. Don't worry, Nancy, I'm a born liar."

They had a time finding the one-man police force of Rabbit Wash. He was asleep in his office and hadn't heard any gunshots recently, but he was reasonably sober, knew Longarm by reputation, and was neighborly about seeing that the dead man would get to the coroner's at the county seat of Scots Wells one of these days. The two law explained that they didn't have a full-time county judge. A circuit judge came by now and again. When Longarm asked who was the coroner at Scots Wells, the town law said it was old Calum MacMillan this year. Longarm sighed and said in that case he could just take his own sweet time and send the rascal over by buckboard when and if they found some ice and rock salt.

Longarm asked if the local lawman had any recent wants on men who shot folk for fun and profit. "The rascal was new to me. I have a fair memory and it would have worked, back there, had I seen a flier on a left-handed gunslick with a scarred lip. He must have caught him a pistol-whipping one time, for now he sneers dead as well as alive."

The Rabbit Wash lawman rummaged some recent yellow sheets from his desk and handed them to the federal deputy and Nancy tugged in desperation on Longarm's sleeve. He turned to her.

She asked, "Can I go now, Custis?"

He said, "We'd best wait until they carry that jasper down your back stairs, Miss Nancy. Your place ain't a place for a delicate-natured female at the moment."

"Good God, I'm not talking about going back *there!*" she said. "I'm leaving Rabbit Wash entire and forever!"

"Well, I can see how being bound and gagged, then witnessing a shootout at close quarters, in one day could leave a lady broody, Miss Nancy. But where would you be thinking of going?"

"Back to Cheyenne, of course. That's where I come from. And that's where I'm going back to! Silas Redford doesn't pay the wages it would take to keep me here, now that someone's gunning for the *Custer County Clarion!*"

Longarm nodded and asked the town law if he had any objections. The older man shook his head. "Nope. The little lady makes a heap of sense. The fewer she-males we has around here to get tied up, the fewer I'll have to worry about."

So the two lawmen headed back to Nancy's to keep her company and tidy up while she packed her carpetbags. The town law said he meant to leave the gent where he was in the closet until he could rustle up some help. He added that he'd never seen the dead man in Rabbit Wash before.

Longarm said, "That's all right. According to this flier, he's well known in Dodge. A hired gun called Lefty Donovan killed a man coming out of the sanitary facilities of the Alhambra less than two weeks ago, according to this flier from Dodge. The description fits. Same split lip, left-handed single-action, and I must say the work sounds familiar."

"Hot damn! Is there a reward on the surly rascal, Longarm?" the town lawman asked.

"There is. The man he shot in Dodge had a rich family as was fond of him. It's a personal reward. You know a federal agent ain't allowed to claim such rewards, don't you?"

"So I heard. Does that mean said reward goes begging, Longarm?"

"Let's talk," Longarm replied, dragging the local lawman into the kitchen as Nancy packed. When they were alone, he said, "Look, the only witness save for myself is leaving town. I doubt she wants to talk about what happened much. She's only leaving because she's scared someone else might come after the *Clarion* and its employees."

"So?"

"So the only coroner for miles around is a pal of mine, and he's in bed with a throbbing head besides. I ain't saying you should bend the truth when you word your official report. Why, that would be downright sinful. But if you saw fit to take credit for bringing this here criminal to justice, you'd be saving me some trouble, and..."

"Never mind all that. Who gets the infernal reward?"

"How the hell should I know? You're the one who's writing up all the paperwork. I'd just as soon not read a word of it, if it's all the same to you. I'll tell you what: you do as you've a mind to. After me and Miss Nancy are gone, you'll have a free hand to do as you feel would best suit the ends of justice. Agreed?"

"Hot damn, Longarm. You sure are a penny from heaven, for it's an election year and—well, you won't mind if I sort of make the Rabbit Wash law look good? It's not like that *reward's* important to me, but..."

Longarm punched him on the shoulder in a friendly way and said, "I know, pard. You and me understand one another entire. So do we even have to bullshit each other?"

Chapter 7

It was almost noon when Longarm loaded Nancy and her carpetbags aboard a northbound passenger train. As long as she was leaving Rabbit Wash forever, Nancy gave him a big wet kiss in public and said she'd never forget him. He said he'd always remember her, too, and asked her to tell Silas Redford to get back pronto if she ran into him in Cheyenne. She said Cheyenne was a mighty big town. But she'd tell him if she met him that his office keys were with the town law and that he owed her for half a week.

When the train rolled out, Longarm asked the old switchman when the next passenger combo was due. It was music to his ears to learn there wouldn't be another before sundown. He'd been worried about Smiley and Dutch getting off the one that had just left.

But as he strode back up the street he reflected that it

was now noon all over, and that Billy Vail would have just about now started to worry about him seriously. Longarm started to head back to the Western Union to see if his boss had put two and two together and wanted to call him a son of a bitch, but he decided not to. If he didn't get orders from his office, how in thunder could anyone expect him to follow them? It was even money that Vail wouldn't send that infernal backup until he had reason to suspicion that his wayward boy was up this way. But Smiley, Dutch, and maybe even the old marshal in the flesh would be arriving by this time tomorrow. That didn't leave Longarm much time to get a handle on the situation.

He went to the one bank in town and asked to speak with the president. The old gent looked pleased to see him until Longarm flashed his badge and told him he didn't have enough money on hand to open an account. He asked the banker what he had to say about Silas Redford depositing how much this morning before he left for Cheyenne. The banker told him it was none of his damned business, but he did say Redford had made a deposit and left on the morning train as Nancy had told him. Longarm considered pressuring the old coot, but decided it wasn't really the federal government's business how much a private citizen might or might not make to put in his own private bank account. He'd heard that over in England the government could tax honest income, but of course such notions would never be allowed on the sensible side of the ocean.

He asked the banker, since he was there, if they had a survey map he could look at. The banker pulled one out of his rolltop and said, "Here—you can keep it. I'm afraid you won't find it too interesting. Custer County is not noted for its natural wonders."

Longarm unrolled the map, nodded, and said, "Lots of pretty grass, though. Are these dotted lines surveyed land boundaries?"

"Of course. What else could be important to a man in the mortgage and loan business out there on the prairie?"

Longarm grinned and said he was much obliged for the copy as he folded it and put it away. The map had the names of landowners neatly printed in each plotted holding. The Double C was a little south of where he'd pictured it.

He went back to unhitch Petunia. The saloon was open now, and he never had gotten fed. He was thirsty, too. But he knew how much time a man could waste in a saloon on jawing, even where there wasn't a gunfight to jaw about. So he led Petunia down to a feed store, bought a bag of oats, and let her water at the trough out front before he let her stick her nose in the feed sack while he held it. When he figured she'd had enough he knotted the bag and lashed it to his saddle. Then he forked himself aboard and said, "Well, old gal, let's go see if them Campbells is as ornery as they want everyone to think."

Petunia was willing, so they made good time for a spell. But as they topped a rise at an easy lope, about a mile from where the map said the Double C's eastern boundary ran, Longarm reined in, surprising Petunia, and dismounted, Winchester in hand. "Go on down and nibble some of that greenup in the bottom of the draw, Petunia," he told the mare. "I suspicion we have us a little shadow, and I'd best see what he wants."

He knew Petunia wouldn't bolt on him, so he paid her no mind as he eased back up the slope he'd just ridden over, crouched low until he neared the top, then dropping to his knees and elbows to cover the rest of the ground Crooked-Lance style.

As he parted the lush grass atop the ridge with the barrel of his saddle gun, another rider on a pinto was walking his mount up the far side, crouching over his saddle swells with a buffalo gun held at port arms. Longarm's Winchester was naturally already armed with a round in its chamber. But he levered a good round of .44-40 out to sound serious as he called out, "Rein in and drop that rifle, friend!"

Some folks just never listened. The startled rider was slick enough to roll out of his own saddle and flop in the grass. But Longarm had half expected him to. So he fired before the other rifleman could get set up. The pinto spooked at the sound of gunfire and ran in one direction as the mysterious stranger's hat went straight up in the sky. Longarm fired into the grass again anyway. Hats usually flew like that when a man was spine shot. But some old boys were tricky sons of bitches.

Longarm rolled away from his own gunsmoke and surveyed the situation for a spell. He could see the blue denim rump of the man in the grass down the slope. The pinto was out of sight. Nobody else seemed to be backing the play of the gent who was presenting his ass as a tempting target. So Longarm took aim and let fly, blowing off a hip pocket and a considerable gout of bloody butt flesh. The man who owned it never moved. Longarm nodded. *I reckon he was spine shot, after all, old son,* he told himself. *It's nice to know someone in this county ain't lying to you, for certain.*

He got up and moved down the slope for a better look at his victim. The big buffalo gun lay in the grass near the downed man's clenched fists. Longarm rolled him over with his booted foot. The rifleman was a total stranger. But Longarm recognized the rifle from the last time it had threatened him with bodily harm. Longarm took out the yellow sheets from the town law in Rabbit Wash as he said, "I surely hope your name ain't Campbell or MacMillan, pard."

The dead man looked hardcased, but he was nondescript. So none of the recent wants told Longarm anything about him. He knelt and fished a wallet from the pocket he hadn't shot off. Aside from fifty-eight dollars in silver certificates, the wallet didn't tell him anything, either. He said to the corpse, "Well, your folks are likely too ashamed of you to want your dead ass shipped home, anyway. Don't go 'way. I'll get us some transportation."

He walked back up and over the rise, stopping along the way to pick up the good round he'd ejected. He saw the pinto grazing down in the draw with Petunia. He smiled.

This day sure is working out right for a change, he told himself.

The pinto looked walleyed but didn't spook as Longarm strode down to the horses, singing them a song about true love. He gathered all the reins, mounted Petunia, and led the pinto back to where its late rider lay dead in the grass. The pinto didn't like it much, but after a little fussing and getting slapped across the eyes with Longarm's hat a few times, the pinto allowed as how it would carry the cadaver facedown and lashed across the saddle. Longarm put the buffalo rifle in its saddle boot while he was at it. He didn't even look for the gent's hat.

About forty-five minutes later he rode in sight of a long, low sod house that had to be the headquarters of the Double C, unless the bank's survey map was a liar, too. As he rode in, a couple of old boys rode out to meet him. They reined in on a rise with the early afternoon sun favoring them from the west. One of them called out, "You're trespassing on posted range, cowboy. You'll ride around, if you know what's good for you."

Longarm didn't answer until he'd gotten within more tolerable voice range. The two proddy hands put their hands to their saddle guns. "Let's not act silly, boys," Longarm called out. "I ain't a cowboy. I'm the law. If you look closer you'll see I'm packing a dead man here. *He* thought he could take me, too, and I'm betting he was a professional killer."

The nearest Double C hand insisted, "We don't care who you are or who that poor unfortunate might have been, Sassenach. Himself has given orders he don't want to be disturbed."

Longarm smiled fondly at them and said, "Well, let's not disturb him with gunfire, then. You boys look like top hands, and good help is hard to find these days since the price of beef has riz. As I was saying, I'm the law, and this murderous bastard was shot on Double C range, or close enough to count as such. It's my aim to carry him in to Scots Wells and see who knows him. Before I do, I might as well see if he ever rode for Duncan Campbell. So that's where we're headed."

He heeled Petunia forward and rode closer, leading the pinto with the dead man across it. The two Double C riders looked soberly at the patent evidence that Longarm wasn't a sissy. But the one doing all the jawing still said, "You can't ride in to the home spread, mister!"

"Sure I can," Longarm said. "It's in plain view, and neither of these ponies has throwed a shoe."

"God damn it, mister, we got *orders!*"

"So have I. I work for the United States Government. And, no offense, President Hayes has to outrank your clan chief by at least a few pay grades."

As he joined them on the rise and obviously meant to ride past them, the less talkative of the two started to draw his saddle gun. He lost interest when he suddenly met the unwinking gaze of Longarm's sixgun. Longarm said, "I'm sorry you made me do that, sonny. Now, suppose the two of you wheel about and ride in ahead of me. I'm getting mighty tired of this tedious conversation, and that poor pinto don't look strong enough to carry *three* dead men!"

The one who'd made the foolish move paled and asked his sidekick, "Rory, what do we do?"

Rory shrugged and replied, "What *can* we do? He's got the drop on us. Let's do like the man says, Donald. We've told him what himself said. It's not our fault if he insists on suicide, is it?"

So they all rode in together, and, from the reception Longarm got, someone had been peering out a window of the ranch house and hadn't liked the view all that much. As they reined in by the east-facing front veranda, a gray old man walking with a cane and flanked by a couple of giants stared morosely at Longarm. "You are on my duthas, sir!" he declared.

One of the hands Longarm had forced to ride ahead called out, "He got the drop on us by surprise, Toshach! We told him not to come here, but, as you see, he's some kind of lunatic!"

Longarm said, "I'm a U. S. federal deputy, too. Before I get around to my other questions, would you take a look at this corpse and tell me if he belongs around here?"

The old chief growled something in the Gaelic and one of the giants ran over to have a look at the dead man. He called back in the same lingo, shaking his head. Duncan the Grim, if that was who it was, said, "He's not one of our own, for which you can thank your maker! Now that you know that, ride on. Nobody here sent for the law, Sassenach."

Longarm dismounted, keeping his .44 in hand but holding it down as he walked closer, saying, "I just told your waddies I'm getting tired of this bullshit. Now I'm telling *you.*"

"Listen here, Sassenach—" the chief began.

But Longarm cut in to snap, "No, God damn it! *You* listen, and listen tight. I was sent up here to tame Scots Wells and the surroundings, and I mean to tame it if I have to blow away bigger frogs than you. You can call me names and you can blow bagpipes at me, for all I give two hoots and a Highland fling. But don't *mess* with me, old man! Two men have tried and two men have died this very day, and I'm starting to feel testy as hell."

The old chief stared hard at Longarm for a long, tense time. Then he smiled thinly and said, "Och, come inside. I like your spirit, lad."

Longarm nodded, turned to the nearest hand, and told him to tether the ponies. The lout replied that he only took orders from his chief. But the chief said something in the Gaelic and he shrugged and did as Longarm had asked.

They went inside. The sod walls had been covered with tooled leather embossed in the curly designs Celts thought pretty. A big round leather shield hung over the fireplace, surrounded by cutlery. Having read an illustrated copy of *The Fair Maid of Perth* as well as *Rob Roy,* Longarm recognized the dirks and claymores as old Scotch weapons. Duncan the Grim waved him to a chair made of elk horns and rawhide as he yelled something awful in the Gaelic before sitting across from Longarm in a wheelchair disguised by a buffalo robe. "Refreshments are due in a minute," he said. "Are you the one they call Longarm? I've heard about you."

Longarm said, "I've heard about you, too, sir. Is it that arthritis crippling your gun hand that makes you hole up out here, so hard to reach?"

The old man looked like someone had spit in his face as he clenched his right fist with considerable pain and effort. "I've plenty of fight left in these old bones, should anyone care to test me!" he snapped.

"I didn't come here to have a fight with you, Mr. Campbell," Longarm said.

"Then watch your manners, you young pup! Aye, I'm not the man I used to be, but I'm still a *man,* for all that. And if you must use a title to go with my proud name, it's not mister, damn it! I prefer to be called An Toshach, or Caen Mhor nan Clann Campbell!"

"I thought the chief of your clan was the Duke of Argyle, in the old country, sir."

"Och, well, we're not in Scotland now, you see."

"I'm starting to. But I never came out here for a Gaelic lesson. They say this latest outbreak of clan warfare was occasioned by one of your kin getting stabbed in the back."

"Ay, and by a MacMillan, I'll stake my life!"

"You may just be doing that, burning crosses and such. I've spoken to Calum MacMillan, and the only difference I can see in your attitudes is that you speak better English."

"Och, that's no great task, when one considers how ignorant those sheep-stealing MacMillans are. Calum didn't speak a word of English before he made love to his first bonny ewe. *I* went to Cambridge."

"I figured you was an educated man. How come you're acting so foolish? The MacMillans say they never killed

MacTavish. They say you boys started it by gunning Sheriff MacMillan."

A pretty young gal came in with a tray. As she placed it on a stand between them Longarm saw that the Campbells drank malt liquor, too. But at least there were some scones between the heroic crystal goblets civilized gents would never dare to fill with anything stronger than wine or cider. He filled the old man in on his conversations with the other side as Duncan the Grim filled their goblets, grim indeed. The old man raised his pint or so of rotgut and said something that sounded like "Slant Eyes." Longarm knew he'd never been mistaken for a Chinese, so he figured it was more Gaelic and said, "Slant eyes yourself" as he picked up his drink and sipped just enough to be polite without committing suicide.

The formalities out of the way, Duncan the Grim got up with an effort, using his cane, and moved over to a curio cabinet in the corner. "I'll show you how I know who killed MacTavish. MacTavish is a sept of Clan Campbell, you must understand."

"Calum MacMillan already told me that, sir. Why are you waving that dagger at me?"

The old chief rejoined him and handed him the highland dirk. "Read what's inscribed on the blade," he said.

Longarm held the dirk up to the light. They hadn't wiped it all that clean after hauling it out of the sheriff's back. So the dried blood in the lettering read easy. But "CUMRICK GHLINNE COMHANN!" meant nothing to Longarm.

"So this is the murder weapon?" Longarm asked. "I don't see MacMillan signed anywhere here, sir."

"Och, you ignorant Sassenach! The message is in the Gaelic, and in the ancient spelling, too! It's Glencoe on the maps now. Cumrick means Remember. So, in full, the message reads, *Remember Glencoe!*"

Longarm nodded in understanding. "I see. It's like 'Remember The Alamo.' Glencoe is where you Campbells did a Santa Anna on another clan, right?"

The old man blanched and thundered, *"Wrong!* God damn all liars! That old slander is a canard and a barefaced lie!"

"You mean you Campbells never massacred nobody at Glencoe?"

"I do. Those were Lowland and English troopers at the Massacre of Glencoe. It's true that Campbell of Glenlyon was in command, but what of it? Shawney Bean *ate* people. But he was a mad loon and an outlaw. Would you blame the Clan MacBean for the behavior of a madman? Campbell of Glenlyon was only the caen of a small branch of our clan. A sub-chief, if you will. Our Toshach Mhor, the Duke of Argyle, never gave orders for the murder of MacIan MacDonald and his people. For God's sake, none of the other Campbell chiefs even knew about it until it was over and done with! The murderous plans were hatched by Lowland politicians. It's said Glenlyon took part in it because MacIan MacDonald was in the habit of stealing his cattle on more than one occasion. But none of the rest of us—"

Longarm raised a hand to stop him before he could really get wound up on old Scotch feuds. He said, "I read *The Fair Maid of Perth,* sir."

Campbell snorted in disgust. "Och, what does Walter Scott know? The Battle of the North Inch of Perth was between Clans MacDhai, or Davidson, and MacPherson. Not Chatten and MacKay, as Scott has it. You see, when MacDhai and MacPherson met the Camerons at Invernahaven—"

"Hold it right there!" Longarm cut in. "I don't *care* if Sir Walter got it right or not. What I'm interested in is how come you say this dagger spells out a murder by a MacMillan or MacMillans unknown. It wasn't the MacMillans as got massacred at Glencoe when Hector was a pup. Now, if you said you suspected someone named *MacDonald* had a mighty long memory for a family grudge..."

"God preserve us from ignorant barbarians!" the old man almost sobbed, going on to explain, "Read your history, lad! Didn't you know *all* the Jacobite clans of the West Highland were allied against the Duke of Argyle? Scratch a MacDonald and a Cameron bleeds. Have a wee bit of fun with a MacPhee lassie and if Lochiel doesn't kidnap your cook, a MacMillan will set fire to your hayrick! They're all thick as thieves. Aye, and all against *us!* The poor misunderstood Clan Campbell has few friends at all in the Highlands!"

"I'm sure you never done nothing to deserve to be so unpopular, sir. I can see how a Campbell might take the writing on this blade as a signed confession by a known enemy. But Calum MacMillan says he knows nothing about it. So let's discuss the murder of the sheriff from *his* side of Main Street."

Campbell shrugged. "I don't know who shot MacMillan in the back, though he doubtless had it coming. If his killer was one of my clan, I give you my word he was acting on his own."

"Is that allowed, sir?" Longarm asked.

"No, but it happens. My people are, I'll admit, prone to hasty judgments and inclined to bloody revenge. A Campbell had been killed, after all. I asked my kinsmen if any of them had done the black deed. For shooting a man in the dark is a black deed, even if he's an enemy. If anyone on our side shot MacMillan, he's ashamed to come forward like a man and admit it."

Longarm asked, "Have you found out who burned that cross on your side of the line last night?"

The old man looked sincerely concerned. "I don't know, and God help him if I ever find out. For the burning rood is a more sacred matter than mere murder. Nobody but the Toshach has the right to order the war beacons lit."

"So I hear tell from the other side. That's why they say you must have ordered it. I'll take your word you didn't, sir. A man would have to be crazy to declare war and then not own up to it. How do you like the notion that some MacMillan did it to tease you Campbells?"

Duncan the Grim hesitated, took another gulp of Scotch whiskey, then shook his head. "In fairness to an old unwashed malignant, Calum the MacMillan would never have ordered Halloween pranks. Like myself, he follows the code. If he lit the cross of war against us, he'd have done so on his side of town. Of course, there's no telling what some young MacMillan loon might have done on his own. Alas, so many of our children have lost the old traditions and become as unruly as you Yankees."

"Yankees and Rebs can both act unruly now and again," Longarm agreed. "That's another question I might as well ask you as long as I'm here, sir," he went on. "I'd already noticed lots of the young folk hereabouts talked like me, despite calling me a sassy knack. How do you clan folks raise your kids in this tradition? Do you read it to 'em out of books, or what?"

The old man shook his head. "You've seen from reading that loon, Walter Scott, that things in books can be wrong. No, the old tales of blood and slaughter are handed down orally. In the old country we had our clan bairds and sennachies, trained to keep the facts correct. I fear, over here, the old ways are dying. We elders try, but once a lad loses his Gaelic and wouldn't know a pipe dirge from a dancing reel—"

Longarm cut in, "That's the point I was after. Half the bully boys in Custer County are as much cowhand as they are clansman. It's starting to look to me as if you older buzzards have been sucked into a needless feud by some troublemakers who don't play by a Scotch gent's rules. I'm likely to see Calum MacMillan, later today, if he survived getting shot in the head."

"Och, I heard Calum was wounded in that skirmish this morning. Do you think he'll live?" the old man asked.

"It's likely. I just said he got shot in the *head*. When I see him, can I tell him that you don't want a war if he don't want a war?"

The old man took another thoughtful swallow of whiskey

before he said, frowning, "Well, that's putting it a bit strongly. I'd not have him think I was suing for peace."

"Can I tell him you won't make the next hostile move? Look, I ain't asking you to run no white flag up your windmill derrick. I just need time to figure out who's behind all this trouble and bring him, them, or whoever to justice. It's against American law to kill sheriffs, no matter what their names might be."

The old man took another sip. Before he could fall on his face, Longarm insisted, "For all we know, MacTavish of Clan Campbell could have been stabbed by some surly gent names Smith or Jones. The same goes for the MacMillan sheriff. I know this comes as a surprise to you, but lawmen do collect enemies like a dog collects fleas. That gent out on the pinto in your dooryard just tried to bushwhack me, and I promise you it was no family feud."

"But the dirk. The inscription..."

"Hell, Chief, I know a dozen mean gents in Denver who'd stab a man in the back for his boots, and half of them can't read English *or* Gaelic! You can see that the dagger is older than hell. Who knows how many pawnshops it might have passed through since some immigrant brought it over from the old country? The inscription fitting an old grudge could be pure accident. Or the murderer could have known a few words of the old lingo and etched it on with acid to throw suspicion on innocent parties."

He rose, swaying unexpectedly as the effects of the malt liquor hit him. "I've got to get that cadaver into town before the sun gets him smelling disgusting," he said. "I'm going to tell the MacMillans you'll be holding your fire for now. I'm holding you to your promise, too!"

The old man stared owlishly up at him and asked, "Promise? Och, what promise? I don't recall making any such promise, lad!"

Longarm said, "Sure you do. I'd watch how much of that stuff I drank at once, Chief. It seems to be making you confused and forgetful as hell."

Chapter 8

Nobody in Scots Wells had any notion who the dead man on the pinto was, either. The only bright spot in his day was that Longarm hadn't yet managed to kill a clansman on either side. Since old Calum MacMillan, the county coroner, had been shot in the head, Longarm took the swelling stiff to the only undertaker in town who wasn't an infernal Scotchman and asked him to keep the body on ice temporarily. He said he would, once Longarm assured him Uncle Sam would pay for his trouble if no kin came forward.

He impounded the pinto for evidence next to Petunia in Fiona's stable, rubbing them both down good and leaving them fodder and water. When he went inside, Fiona was crying.

He asked her how come and she said, "Och, ye'll nae want to stay wi' me this nicht, my love."

He said, "Sure I will," hoping he was man enough. He'd forgotten how passionate the Scotch gal was, while making love to old Nancy. Fiona looked up at him with an expression of adoring regret and said, "I'm coming doon wi' the curse of womankind! I wasna' expecting it so early this month."

He managed to look concerned instead of relieved as he bent over, kissed her, and soothed, "Hell, is that all that's upsetting you?"

"Och, isn't it enough, you daft brute? I ken the sort of mon ye are. I ken ye'll be casting eyes on other women before yon sun ha' set, noo that ye know *I* canna service ye tonicht!"

He sat down across the kitchen table from her and reached out to take her hand. "You didn't service me last night, honey. You screwed me, and damned good. But, hell, there's more to being pals than slap and tickle. Ain't we still pals, Fiona?"

"Och, do ye mean ye'll not abandon my bed for another's, even if we have to abstain?"

"Well, we'd best sleep like brother and sister, a ways apart, lest I wake up in the middle of the night and start doing what comes natural before we're awake."

She laughed like a kid who'd just been given a new and delightful toy. "I think ye mean that! Och, Custis, I was sae afraid ye'd leave me when I had to confess my shame."

"The way nature messes you gals up every month is a raw deal from Creation, but it ain't anything to be ashamed about, Fiona. You've knowed from the start I can't stay here forever, but, as long as I'm here in Scots Wells, we'll work something out. You're still the prettiest gal in town, and a mighty fine cook, too!"

She cooed with delight and leaped up to start making something for him to eat. He regarded her fondly as she scrambled some eggs and fried some potatoes. He was hungry as a wolf and meant what he'd said about her cooking. He was holed up good with a gal who kept lavender in her linen closets and kept her mouth shut about his comings and goings as well. The last thing he needed, at least tonight, was another back-breaking orgy. So far, he'd had better luck at getting laid up here than at anything else.

He wolfed down the late noon dinner as Fiona stared at him lovingly. Then he looked at his watch. "I got some chores to tend, little darling. I'll try to get back in time for supper. If I'm tied up, don't wait hungry. I often has to eat on the fly."

"Ay, but when wi' ye be cooming home?"

"If I knew, I'd have just told you, honey lamb. Don't look at me so confused. Nobody around here is more confused than me."

He got up from the table and she walked him to the back door to kiss him goodbye. He kissed her tenderly and tweaked her breast to show her they were still pals. He was thankful she couldn't take him up on it. Between all the riding, including horses, and all the hard liquor he'd consumed during duty hours, he felt he couldn't have gotten it up again with a block and tackle.

He walked to the end of the alley and cut over to the main street. He meant to go next to the house in town where they had Calum MacMillan bedded down. But as he strode along the walk on the MacMillan side of the street, a frosty-looking old gent in a suit he must have stolen from a scarecrow seemed intent on blocking his path. Longarm stopped, polite, and the older man said, "I am the Reverend Hamish Bell, pastor of the Kirk of the Resurrection."

That sounded mighty important, so Longarm nodded. "Howdy, Reverend. I seen your church, if it's the one to the west side of the square. It's a mighty handsome building, at least from the outside."

"Aye, that's what I wanted to talk to you about, young man. I didn't see you in my kirk on the Lord's Day. What have you to say for yourself about that?"

Longarm was tempted to tell the preacher he was a Muslim, but that didn't seem respectful, so he smiled and said,

"You didn't see me at your services because I wasn't there, Reverend."

"Och, do you mean to tell me you attended services at the High Kirk with Clan Campbell?" the pastor exclaimed.

"Not guilty. That's the one with the taller steeple, glaring at yourn across the green, right?"

"It is. The High Kirkers have ever been vainglorious. But if you didn't go to the Low Kirk and you didn't go to the High Kirk..."

"I'd have been in Scotland afore you, if I'd been to any Scotch church at all. I never got here until late Sunday afternoon, Reverend. I went to church in Denver earlier," Longarm lied.

"Did you now? Well, I'm *waiting,* man!"

"Excuse me? Waiting for what, Reverend?"

"The name of your religious affiliation, of course! You must go to *some* kirk, even though I see you reek of the creature even this early in the day!"

Longarm repressed an annoyed retort, since he already had somebody local gunning for him. "You don't *see* the malt liquor on my breath, Reverend," he said. "You *smell* it. Let's keep things accurate if we has to stick our noses into other folks' business. Since you asked polite, I'll tell you true I go to service and sometimes a Sunday-Go-to-Meeting-on-the-Green at the First Church Of Farther-Along-We'll-Know-All-About-It-and-Hard-Shell-Holy-Rolling in the saintly city of Denver, Colorado."

The busybody sniffed and said, "I've never heard of any such kirk."

Longarm shrugged and answered, "We don't mind. Nobody in Denver ever heard of *your* church, neither. Now that you know I ain't a Mormon or a runaway nun, is there anything else I can do for you, Reverend? I'd offer to buy you a drink, but you look tough and it's too hot to fight."

"I don't defile my body with strong spirits, thank you. You didn't say where you were staying here in Scots Wells, did you?"

"By gum, you're right. I didn't. I ain't interested in where *you* bed down, neither."

"Are you evading an answer to my question, young man?"

"I sure am. Considering your lack of humor, you seem mighty observant, Reverend. Can we talk about the feud in these parts? Since you know I came to town on the Sabbath, you likely know why. I'm a lawman sent to catch me some murderers. Since you keep tabs on where everyone comes and goes in this town, who do you have down as the killer of either sheriff?"

The preacher stared aghast and said, "Do I look like I consort with murderers, young man?"

"Not hardly. You don't look like you screw around and you just said you don't drink either. But you sure are mighty interested in them as does. I'll tell you what let's do, Reverend. I'll tell you if I suspicion anyone of having a deck of cards in his or her house and you tell me as soon as you find out who's been stirring up *real* trouble in these parts, all right?"

The nosy preacher stood there gaping like a fish out of water as he tried to determine if he'd been insulted or, worse yet, laughed at. Longarm nodded pleasantly and stepped around him to walk on. He knew that if old Bell knew anything a sensible lawman could possibly be interested in, he'd have thundered it from his pulpit by this time.

The head-shot Calum MacMillan was bedded down in the spare room of Doc Essex, the only doctor in town trusted by both clans, since he was a sassy knack who didn't know how to play old war tunes on a bagpipe. The doc's wife let Longarm in and led him back to where the old chief sat propped up in bed with his head wrapped like a Hindu and a mess of younger men gathered around him like the shepherds in the manger.

They were mostly dressed cow, but stared down at their old chief as if they'd bet even money he could walk on water or cure disease.

The one standing with his head nearest the ceiling was

Angus Bethune, of course. When Longarm asked old Calum how he felt, Bethune said, "Our Toshach will live—no thanks to those treacherous Campbells. I've issued a personal challenge to their champion, Gordie Thompson, to meet me man to man at a time and place of his choosing."

"Oh, shut up," Longarm said. "Chief MacMillan, can we talk private? I brought you a message from Duncan the Grim, and children should be seen and not heard."

The big Bethune paled around the lips and said softly, "That's a mortal insult to my manhood, Sassenach! Would you care to step outside this sickroom and repeat it?"

The old chief snapped something in the Gaelic and Bethune shrugged, growled, "Later, Long," and headed out of the room. Those of the others who didn't have the Gaelic at least had sense enough to follow his drift.

When they were alone, the man in bed stared up soberly at Longarm. "So ye've brought me a taunt fra' the Campbell?" he asked. "Well, oot wi' it, lad. I won't hold ye responsible for the ravings of a madman."

Longarm took out two cheroots, handed one to MacMillan, and lit them both up before he said, "Duncan the Grim did talk as crazy as you. But he says he didn't order the killing of Sheriff MacMillan and he has no notion who burned that cross last night. Your turn."

The old man grinned like a wolf and asked, "Are they begging for peace, then? On what terms?"

Longarm said, "Betting is putting it a mite strong. Let's say Campbell seems willing to hold his fire for now. The terms is Mexican standoff. They won't attack you if you don't attack them. I'd take 'em up on it. If you hadn't been wearing that belt buckle on your hat instead of where it belongs, you'd be dead right now."

The old man put a thoughtful hand to his bandaged head. "I've stopped seeing double and it only hurts when I shake my head hard," he said. "I'll be up and aboot by this time tomorrow. And if ye met Grim Duncan ye saw the auld loon is half crippled, however much he tries to hide it by skulking in his grand hoose."

Longarm made a mental note that if MacMillan thought that big but soggy old soddy was a mansion, his own spread in the foothills couldn't be much to look at. But he said aloud, "Look, now that I've met both of you, I've concluded that you're both cross-grained old coots. But you both seem to be decent old gents who've been sucked into this foolishness by someone out to make trouble behind your backs."

"They started it. Nae man of my clan would have gunned Sheriff MacMillan!"

"We've rid over that range. The trouble starts with someone putting that fancy blade in a MacTavish from the other side. Let's get caught up on who's been murdered since. Down in Denver I was told folks have been dying like flies up here. But, so far, the only names I have are the two sheriffs. Who got killed after MacMillan?"

The old man frowned and replied, "After poor Angus MacMillan was shot doon like a dog fra' behind his back? Och, nobody, ye loon. We were *working* on that when ye showed up to interfere wi' our auld customs!"

Longarm blinked in surprise and gasped, "Jesus Christ! You mean to tell me the total score of this clan war stands at two men? Hell, I've shot two since I've been here, and I only just arrived! My office has it down that you Scotchmen are locked in mortal combat up here in Custer County, with bullets flying every which way and... Hold the thought. I have seen women and children on the streets of Scots Wells since I got here. But then, who told the Justice Department things was as serious as I was led to believe?"

The old man shrugged. "I dinna ken. Some outsiders were up here earlier than ye, talking daft aboot us voting Democrat or Republican in some election. Everyone in Custer County votes MacMillan or Campbell. Sae some bullets flew indeed until the Sassenachs got the message they had no business here. But the lads were only having fun. Nobody drew blood from those wee politicoos."

Longarm took out his notebook and pencil, muttering, "All right. I see now that nothing Marshal Vail told me counts."

The old man brightened and asked, "Was that Vail ye said? Och, why did ye not tell us ye worked for a mon wi' a bonny Jacobite name?"

Longarm frowned. "Billy Vail ain't no such thing. He's from Texas," he told the Scotsman.

"Ay, but the MacVails are a sept of Clan Cameron, and MacMillan stood by Cameron at the battle of Culloden, ye ken."

"Oh, put your bagpipes away and let's talk sensible! Billy Vail may have a Scotch name, though I reckon it would surprise the hell out of him to hear it. Everybody has to have a name from *some* old country unless he's an Indian. If my boss was at all interested in this Celtic mythology I'd have heard about it by now. Forget Billy Vail and everything that took place anywhere before this particular feud started. How did you folk get along up here before someone knifed that first sheriff, MacTavish?"

"Warily," replied the old man. "We all coom together to work for the Amalgamated British Beef Trust, back in the Seventies. Ye see, they had the grand notion that Highland cattle—"

"Skip that part and move up to more recent," Longarm cut in.

"Och, ye make it hard for a man to carry on a decent conversation if ye dinna want details. Verra well. When we were left here to fend for our ainsels the Campbell and me had a word and a drink on how we were to divide up the country. This toon sits fair in the middle. Sae it was agreed no Campbell would file a homestead claim to the west and we in turn would leave the eastern half of the range to them."

"What about the other folks in the county?" Longarm asked.

"Who are ye talking about, lad? There's nobody here but

us, unless ye count a few odd Sassenachs like Dr. Essex here. He'll tell ye we Scots have never bullied nor bothered anyone unfortunate enought to have been born a poor clanless loon. The few Sassenachs and Arapaho breeds as we have among us enjoy the same rights as any decent mon, as lang as they act decent. We ootnumber them twa or more to one, but we're a bonny live-and-let-live race."

"I've noticed," Longarm replied. "All right. You divvied up the range and I can see who does business on which side of Main Street. How in thunder could you divvy up the running of the county? You do run this county, *some,* don't you?"

"We did until yon Campbells started playing us false. Ye've seen the county courthoose. The circuit judge is a Sassenach, but a decent fair-minded mon, and he hardly cooms aroond in any case. As to local positions, it was agreed we'd divide them justly between our clans. I took the high office of county coroner. Angus MacTavish of Clan Campbell was made the sheriff to balance the affairs of justice. The other county positions were filled the same way."

"Hold on—wasn't there ever any *elections?*"

The old man looked sincerely puzzled. "What would be the sense of holding elections, even if that was our custom? Any mon can see that wi' every MacMillanite voting wi' me and every Campbell mon voting wi' Duncan the Grim, any election would be a tie, or so close to a tie we'd ever be in the Statehoose demanding a recounting of the ballots. Nae, lad, it made more sense to do it the auld Highland way."

Longarm shrugged and said, "All right, so the balance was upset when someone murdered the sheriff the Campbells picked. Who picked Angus MacMillan to replace him?"

"I did, of course. As county coroner it was my right."

"And you say the Campbells had no reason to suspicion your side of stabbing their sheriff? You should have held a proper election, damn it. The whole point of democracy is to avoid suspicions of favoritism!"

"So those Republican and Democrat loons fra' Denver said. But I just told ye, Yankee-style elections would only confuse things worse here in Custer County. Anyone can see each clan controls half the votes up here. Besides, as I said, it's not our custom to decide wha's right or wrong by asking the opinion of every lowborn loon. The English have never understood that aboot us. That's the reason we Jacobites were ever rising after the fools in London told us William and Mary, not James Stuart, was our rightful monarchs."

"Stop right there. I don't want to hear one word about no college back East. I've got the picture. You folks are more comfortable letting some old chief decide things for you. At least, *some* of you are. But it just comes to me that any number of younger men raised more American could be intent on changing the status quo by getting both you and Duncan the Grim shot. This morning it almost worked. You're in bed with a head wound and Duncan the Grim is holed up with his gun hand crippled. Was either Gordie Thompson or Angus Bethune born on this side of the pond? They both talk as American as me."

The old man scowled and snapped, "I'll not have the Bethune lad slighted! It's true he grew to manhood over here, but he was born wi' the Gaelic on his tongue in Bonny Lochaber! He's a good true lad as well as foreman of my Double M. As to Gordie Thompson—well, he is a Campbell, but Scotland born, for a' that. He'd not do anything against the orders of auld Duncan. But who's to say what orders a *Campbell* would give?"

Longarm put his notebook away, as confused as before. "I asked you to stop jawing at me about ancient history. It's dead and buried. I'm here to keep other folks from winding up the same way before their appointed time. I thank you for such information about the here and now as you can remember. Now I have to head back to Rabbit

106

Wash to see what a plain American has to say about some mysterious doings at his newspaper office. Before I go, I've got one last question. Ain't it true that before all this feuding and fussing started, you and old Duncan Campbell was friends?"

"Och, the mon's a *Campbell!* Whatever gave ye the idea we could ever be more than neighbors respecting an armed truce?" the old man cried.

"Respect is the word I should have said. Friend may have been putting it too strong. But I got the impression Duncan Campbell still respects you, at least. He told me he didn't think you could have ordered some of the sillier things as has been going on," Longarm said.

Calum MacMillan's eyes softened and he almost smiled as he asked, "Och, did he, noo? Well, it's only right that even my enemies do me justice. Since he's willing to admit my gentle breeding, I'll concede yon Campbell has ever kept his gi'en word. But he's still an auld bastard, and ye can tell him I said so when ye see him!"

Longarm laughed, said he would, and left the sickroom, consulting his watch. It was mid-afternoon, now. If he and Petunia hurried, and the night train from Cheyenne ran on time, he could make it back before midnight and get a night's sleep—alone, for a change.

Outside, big Angus Bethune was waiting for him, alone, but blocking the walk as Longarm swung out of the doc's gate to head for Fiona's stable.

"I'll have a word with you now about children being seen and not heard," Bethune said.

Longarm said, "No, you won't. I'm in a hurry. Got to get to Rabbit Wash and back, and it looks like rain before midnight."

"You'll go noplace until you apologize or fill your fist, you Sassenach son of a bitch?"

Longarm smiled thinly up at Bethune—a rare position for the tall deputy to find himself in. "Let's see, now," he said. "If I called you a child and you called me a son of a bitch, I'd say you were ahead on insults. So why don't we leave her there, pard?"

"If ye won't fight with guns, would you like to settle it man to man with fists?"

"Do I look like a total fool? You've got forty pounds and a foot or so of reach on me, Bethune! I'll shoot you later if you like. But I can't do it right now. Like I said, I'm in a hurry and on government business."

He stepped around the young giant and strode on as, behind him, Bethune called out, "Coward! You've no right to show your face in broad day, you grinning sheep-fucker!"

Longarm let that one bounce off his back. But this sure was getting tedious. He swung the first corner as Bethune stood there shouting taunts after him. He made his way back to Fiona's, saddled Petunia up, and rode down the alley to the far end of town before he cut across the rear of the county courthouse and headed east again.

He decided, since he'd been trailed on the wagon trace and again on the rises south of it, to try his luck by riding well north of the wash and wagon trace this time. He couldn't get lost on the high plains with the sun shining, once he knew where the important places were.

But as he reined in on a rise and glanced back to see if any company was coming, he noticed the western horizon was starting to look mighty broody. He told Petunia, "I was wrong, old gal. We'll play hell getting back before it rains fire and salt on the lone prairie. Them clouds above the Front Range hint at one gully-washing spring storm long before midnight. Oh, well—I got my slicker tied to the cantle behind me, and you walk about naked anyways."

Chapter 9

Nothing seemed to be following them but the threatening storm. So they rode on, taking their time. Longarm didn't really have to be in Rabbit Wash this side of sundown and it was a short ride once you knew the way. He was starting to feel almost human again. Riding was almost as restful as just sitting and whittling, and the hearty vittles Fiona had fed him had soaked up the effects of the malt liquor on an empty gut. He reminded himself to stick to beer or, at the most, needled beer as he killed time waiting for Redford's train from Cheyenne. He meant to be at the siding, and forted some, well before Redford arrived. For if folks were worried about something being printed in the *Clarion,* and it hadn't been set in type, they might suspicion it was in Silas Redford's head. Longarm aimed to make sure nobody blew said head off the publisher's shoulders before they talked it over some.

Petunia started to spook, but steadied as a tumbleweed came over a rise to roll past them headed west at considerable speed. Longarm said, "Oh-oh, that storm above the mountains figures to be even worse than I thought, Petunia. Thunderation and a little hail is only to be expected this time of the year. But unless that storm has a twister or more in its teeth it wouldn't be sucking in the ground air so soon."

He shrugged and rode on. In truth, a tornado presented less danger to a mounted man on open prairie than lightning did. A man on a sensible mount could easily sidestep a twister coming over the horizon at them. But lightning tended to strike the tallest object around when it struck at all. So a man sitting tall in the saddle had to look sharp indeed if he aimed to sidestep a lightning bolt.

Greenhorns were always getting struck by lightning on the high plains. Back East, the sky tended to warn ahead by brooding up all cloudy and dark before the first bolts hit. The western sky was notorious for what was somewhat poetically called a bolt from the blue. Many a poor pilgrim had been fried in his saddle, surprised as he rode along a ridge under what he thought was a cloudless sky. Longarm wasn't a pilgrim any more, so he said, "Petunia, we'd best find up a nice low draw trending east. Now that I study on it, the old sun ball's looking sort of fuzzy around the edges."

He swung farther north. He knew the dry wash Rabbit Wash was named for lay to the south. He knew a sandy bottom meant it flash flooded with every rain, too.

They topped a rise and he saw a wide, shallow draw spread out below them. It was paved with short grass and ran east and west. Someone else must have figured it was above dangerous flooding, too. A bitty sod house surrounded by a pole corral full of ponies was set against the north rise of the draw. The homestead lay to Longarm's east, so he had to pass it to get to the railroad town. As he headed that way, he noticed the ponies in the corral were milling and the laundry hanging from the line running between the house and a corral post was flapping fit to bust loose and play tumbleweed. He wondered why the homesteaders weren't battening down the hatches. There were windows in the sod walls. Couldn't they see it was fixing to blow like hell?

Apparently they couldn't. As he rode closer there wasn't a sign of life from the soddy, even as the situation deteriorated outside all around. A young chestnut colt took a running jump at the corral gate, made it halfway over, then fought its hung-up hind legs free and was off and running in the general direction of Mexico.

Longarm heeled Petunia into a lope almost without thinking. The old cutting horse knew the rules on runaway stock, too, and dashed forward at the right angle to cut the fool colt off as it crossed the draw, wide-eyed and bawling like a branded calf.

Longarm wasn't packing a throw rope on his McClellan saddle. He'd have looked foolish trying to rope from a hornless army saddle and he hadn't come put here to work stock anyway. But a man did what a man had to do, and it wasn't neighborly to let stock run off unescorted.

Petunia cut the colt off on the south slope of the draw as Longarm waved his hat in its face and said, "Hold on, horse. You're going the wrong way!"

The colt tried to get around Petunia with a sneaky shift of his weight, but Petunia was older and wiser. She butted him with her chest to turn him sideways, then bit him on the rump to head him back down the slope. He didn't like it much, but every time he tried to turn, Petunia cut him off and nipped him some more. So, like it or not, they got him headed back to the homestead.

Longarm was wondering how in hell he was going to open the gate to herd the fool colt back in when a chubby little red-headed gal in a calico Mother Hubbard ran out of the house, skirts whipping in the wind, to open the gate ahead of them. One of the other ponies tried to take advantage of the opening, but the redhead shooed him back from the gate by flapping her skirts at him. She flapped them high and gave Longarm a better look at her plump bare legs than she might have intended.

The colt they were hazing in bolted into the corral, relieved to get his rump away from Petunia's teeth, although in truth she hadn't broken the skin enough to matter. Longarm reined in as the redhead swung the gate shut and called out, "Och, God bless you, sir! I was afraid when I saw you out yon window that you might be a MacMillan. But when I saw you were a gentleman about a poor widow woman's wee daft horsie..."

Longarm ticked the brim of his Stetson as he smiled down at her and said, "I only done what was right, ma'am. As you can see, it's fixing to blow, and mayhaps even twist. I got places to go, but if you need help in tying things down, I'm at your beck and call. My name is Custis Long and I works for the U. S. A. If you're worried about MacMillans, you'd likely be a Campbell, right?"

"Aye, I'm Sine MacTavish, the poor lone widow of himself, the late Sheriff Andrew MacTavish. But come inside where we can talk out of this wind!"

He surely wanted a word with her, now that he knew who she was. "You go on in and I'll join you after I gather your wash and secure them ponies," he said.

She started to object. Then a gust of wind lifted her thin calico skirt up around her waist and he could see she wasn't wearing a thing under it. She was red-haired all over. She blushed as red as her hair as she shoved her skirts down and ran inside.

Longarm dismounted and led Petunia over to the corral. He tied the reins over the front swells of his McClellan, opened the gate again, and put her inside, saying, "I'm sorry, Petunia. I know you'd feel better on the lee side of the house. But I want you to stay here and make these other children behave."

He knew she would. He could see she enjoyed bossing

colts and he knew she had more sense than to run off into a gathering storm saddled and bridled. The wind tried to steal his hat as he headed to rescue the widow woman's washing, but Longarm put a hat on cavalry style, to stay.

He gathered the flapping wash in on big bundle and headed for the house. Sine MacTavish had been watching out a window and she opened the door for him. She needed his help to close it against the gusts. As they bolted it against the howling outside, she gasped with relief. *"Och, mo mala! Do you think the roof will stay with us long enough for high tea?"*

He glanced up at the lodgepole pine rafters. "We're safe for anything this side of a twister, ma'am," he assured her.

"Aye, but what if a tornado comes?"

"We wind up dead or alive, depending on where it puts us down."

"That's no way to cheer a frightened lassie, Custis Long. But I do feel safer now that you're here. You will be staying until the storm is over, won't you?"

He hesitated, then said, "I'll stay a spell, ma'am. At least till the wind dies down. Don't hold me to staying through the rain, though. I'm on government business, and it might not be decent. It figures to rain all night."

She dimpled, blushed, and started hauling the one small table in the one-room soddy closer to the bed. He studied and saw her intent when he noticed there was only one chair. "One sits on yon bed," she said. "It had best be you, since I must be back and forth from the range."

He saw she already had a fire in the kitchen range, which took up most of the far wall. It looked dumb, in springtime, but he knew that when a blue norther blew down across the high plains in January it would take all that stove had to offer to keep things comfortable in here.

He took off his hat, hung it on a wooden peg driven into the sod wall, and eased around to sit gingerly on the bedstead at the head of the table. The late Sheriff MacTavish had likely eaten lots of dinners like this. It must have saved time later. The bedsprings were oiled silent and the redhead sure filled that thin calico out temptingly. She was a mite plumper than Longarm liked his women, but she wasn't his woman and she wasn't *too* plump.

As she bustled over her range with the fixings for high tea, he noticed she didn't need a bustle to fill out behind like a Flora Dora Gal, either. He felt a slight tingle where no sensible man had a right to tingle after all he'd been through in recent memory. He silently told his fool pecker to behave. He didn't have the time, even if he didn't suspect it was just showing off. There was nothing as could make a man feel sillier than a half-hard pecker and a new gal expecting more from a decent gent.

As she made high tea and small talk with her back to him, Longarm could tell she'd gotten over the first shock of widowhood. MacTavish had been dead long enough for her to flirt some with her body movements. He wondered if she knew she was doing it. Maybe she just shifted her weight like that on her bare feet and naked legs because she had considerable weight to shift. She was about two inches shorter and six inches wider across the hips than Fiona, and Fiona was built more hourglass than old blonde Nancy. He wondered if Nancy would meet up with someone in the wicked city of Cheyenne tonight, instead of remembering him forever as she'd promised. It wasn't right for a healthy young gal to feel left out. That was one of the reasons Longarm always tried to console widow women as best as he was able.

By the time Sine brought the tea and scones with marmalade to the table, Longarm had a full erection. To take his mind off it, he said, "I can see you're able to talk about your late husband's passing, ma'am. I know better than to bring up gory details at table. But I told you I was law. So would it distress you to answer me just a few questions about the case?"

"The MacMillans killed Andrew with a Clan Donald curse on the blade," she said simply as she stuffed her mouth with dough and jam. She had a pretty little rosebud mouth, but it was easy to see from the way she inhaled the marmalade and scones why she was getting a double chin under it.

"I know all about the old Highland dirk, ma'am," he said. "I got some other questions. For instance—no offense, but anyone can see that you and your late husband lived on a modest homestead miles from town. Did he ride in every day to the Scots Wells sheriff's office from here?"

She washed down her food with a gulp of tea before she replied. "Not every day. Just when someone sent for him. Before the feud started again, there was little work for a sheriff here in Custer County. The toshachs didn't allow much trouble, you see."

Longarm swallowed a modest piece of scone and a sip of tea. The marmalade and tea were both a mite too sweet. He studied as he chewed and swallowed, then said, "Right. The almost-honorary coroner's position was filled by a gent whose real business is raising beef. They told me your husband was killed in town. Am I upsetting you?"

"No, I already knew Andrew was dead. We buried him months ago. He was killed in town. On the walk between the Thistlegorm and the town square. They found him, stark in the morning dew, on the walk the next morning. I'd been wondering what was keeping him all night. But—well—Andrew did tend to neglect his duties at home when he'd been at the creature."

"You're saying that he was inclined to drink, ma'am?"

"Inclined? *Och, mo mala,* he drank anything in any position! It's not that I don't miss Andrew, you ken. He was a good man when he was here, and it's fair lonely I live since he's gone. But, in truth, he was the town drunk. Didn't anyone in Scots Wells tell you that?"

Longarm frowned. "No. I reckon you folks wash your own dirty linen. So, let's see, now. We have us a drinking man who don't take his job serious, riding miles across empty prairie on the rare occasions he goes to work. Yet

115

they kill him in *town?* Why in thunder should they take such a chance? Has anyone ever considered that someone might have stabbed the wrong gent? It was dark, and he had his back to his murderer, right?"

"If you say so." She shrugged, stuffing another scone in her mouth whole. He wondered idly how she managed it. She swallowed the heroic mouthful with the help of her tea, poured some more in her cup, and gasped for air as she added, "I think they *wanted* him found on the streets of Scots Wells with that dirk in him, as a warning."

"Let's not talk about the Massacre of Glencoe, please. Can you think of a more sensible motive for anyone killing a man named MacTavish?"

"Well, he had been drinking in the Thistlegorm that night."

Longarm started to ask a dumb question. Then he nodded and said, "Oh, right—Campbell clansmen was supposed to belly up to the bar in the Argyle Arms. Did he have words with any of the regulars in the MacMillan-haunted saloon, ma'am?"

She reached a plump hand out for another scone as she answered. "I don't know. I wasn't there. It's not seemly for women to drink in either saloon. I don't remember hearing of Andrew having an argument in the Thistlegorm. He was ever a friendly lad, drunk or sober, and our clans were not at feud that night."

Longarm declined to drop it for now. He was putting this case together an inch at a time as he jawed with folks. But he didn't need inches. He needed the end of the bolt, before Billy Vail got that night letter and saddled him with a posse of even more confused lawmen.

He finished his tea, politely refused a second cup, and glanced out the window near the head of the bedstead. "The wind seems to be letting up now. I'd say this is the lull before the storm. If I leave now I ought to make it to Rabbit Wash before the rain hits."

"Please don't go." She sighed, and explained, "You're the first company I've had in days, and it's so lonely out here, now that I'm forced to sleep alone."

He said cautiously, "Just give yourself some time, Sine. You're a handsome woman and I see you no longer wear widow's weeds."

She pouted her rosebud mouth. "I'm expected to when I go to kirk in town. No man of my clan will come near me until Andrew has been in the ground at least a year and a day."

"Oh, well, are you allowed to spark with other gents, ma'am?"

"Och, what other gents *are* there in this county? Would you have me kiss a *MacMillan? Och, no mala*, I'd sooner make love to a goat!"

Longarm's glands reacted more to the randy turn the conversation was taking than his more sensible parts did. It wasn't the words the redhead was saying as much as the way she was sending him signals with her big green eyes that made him tingle when he didn't have time to tingle.

She must have felt tingly, too, for she blushed and sprang up to clean the table and drag it back to the middle of the rammed earth floor. Longarm tried to come up with a polite way to say he was leaving, come hell or high water.

He rose to his feet, stared out the window, and said, "Yep, I see by the grass stems that the wind has died total, now. I thank you kindly for the high tea Miss Sine. But me and Petunia has some ground to cover before dark, so—"

"You can't go yet!" she said firmly, moving to block the door bodily with her attractive but considerable form.

He smiled down at her. "Sure I can, if only you'll let me by, ma'am. Look, it ain't that I don't admire your company, but I got to meet the Cheyenne night train."

"It won't be dark for hours. Surely you can stay just a little while? Och, Custis, I've been so *lonely!*"

His voice was gentle as he answered. "I can see that, ma'am. I know the feeling and it hurts, even when you're a man. I'd stay an hour or more if I thought it would really help, but it wouldn't, Miss Sine. I have to meet that train and you'd only wind up alone here in any case."

She looked away, licked her pink rosebud lips, and murmured, "At least stay long enough to lay me. I'm sure I'd be able to sleep tonight if only some man would throw a good come into me!"

He blinked in astonishment, tried to come up with a polite answer, then, since he couldn't, he just slipped off his coat, tossed it on the table with his gun rig, and reeled her in for a consoling kiss.

She kissed back, love-starved as a mare in heat, and started hauling up her skirts with one hand as she fumbled at his buttons with the other. He came up for air and said, "Wouldn't it work better in the bed?" So she pulled free with a giggle, slipped the Mother Hubbard off over her red head, and leaped aboard the bedstead, stark naked and blushing all over. He didn't want her to feel embarrassed being naked alone in broad day, so he sat down beside her and finished peeling his own duds off.

By the time he rolled aboard her in the same shameless condition, the redhead was moaning and rolling her plump curves under him like a marshmallow sea. Her eyes were closed and she rolled her head from side to side, pleading, "Hurry! Don't tease me, you brute!"

He said, "I'm trying, little darling, but you'd best hold still long enough for me to find the way home!"

She reached down between them to help him, gasped when she took what he had to offer in her little plump hand, and said, "Lords and ladies! Is all that meant for poor wee *me?*"

But she wasn't as scared as she let on. For she raised her plump pink body to meet his as she guided the head into her gushing love box and swallowed him alive.

Longarm groaned as he felt how soft she was on the inside as well. Her plump thighs felt like satin pillows hugging his hips as he settled well in the saddle to ride. And, thanks to the well-endowed rump of the randy redhead, they needed no pillow under her to do it hard and deep. From the way she was moving and moaning he could tell that was the way she wanted it. So, since he was in a hurry in any case, he just let go and pounded her good.

Thanks to his earlier adventures that day, he couldn't come in her as soon as an active gal like this would have made him had he started the game with a fresh deck. He had no trouble keeping it up, and her soft, smooth flesh inspired him to try hard. But he was concerned that she might not think he liked her as he screwed on and on without much result.

Fortunately, she took it as a compliment, if she thought about *his* orgasms at all. Sine MacTavish made love the way she ate — with a healthy appetite and little concern for the crumbs. She gasped and cried out in Gaelic as he could tell by her contractions that she was coming so hard it must have hurt some. So he faked an orgasm. It was a she-male trick a friendly gal in Dodge had let him in on when he was still young and foolish. As they lay limp together he said, "You're going to have to talk American if you expect sensible answers, honey box."

She laughed and said, "Did I lapse into the auld tongue, then? Well, it's small wonder, for I've not been laid like that since before I wed Andrew. It was a great day indeed when you came into my life, you wondrous man. I know you can't stay the night. But can we do it some more by the bonny light of day? Och, I feel so naked and so gloriously shameful, rutting like a wee beastie. Don't you?"

He laughed. "Well, since you seem in a show-off mood, we may as well get good and dirty."

He rolled off her and picked her up from the bedstead. She asked why he'd taken it out. Then, when he placed her plump rump on the plank table in the center of the room, she laughed and lay back across it. "So that's the plan, is it? Verra well. This wee table will ever remind me of pleasanter things than eating!"

He stood upright as he picked up a softly padded knee with each hand and pulled her on again like a glove. She hissed and said, "Och, it goes so deep this way!" as he started moving again. That had only been part of the plan. His usual screwing muscles were getting stiff for some reason, and the change of position helped. She moaned and spread her thighs wider. "Can you see it? Can you see it going in and out of me?" she asked.

He said he sure could, as he also noticed he could see out the window standing here. The sky outside was still clear. The wind had died down total. But from the way the sun was slanting on the grass he figured to ride into Rabbit Wash after sundown, even if he started now.

His abstraction, coupled with his automatic posting in the saddle, conspired to make her come again ahead of him. He didn't mind. Doing it in this position was sort of like posting at a trot, and any old cavalry trooper could keep this up indefinitely. The redhead gasped. "My Lord, is there no end to your lust, you marvelous monster? How many times have we come together?"

"I've lost count," Longarm lied.

She didn't answer. She was coming again, and the table was never meant to bear all that weight bouncing all over it. He slid his palms along the backs of her thighs to hold some of Sine off the table lest it collapse under her. She arched her spine as he lifted her behind off the edge and groaned, "Have mercy! It's the bottom you're hitting with every stroke and . . . Ohhhh never mind what I just said. I'm coming!"

Longarm could see she was. Her plump chest was heaving and he was starting to feel sort of left out. He knew he'd never forgive himself if he left without even coming in her once. But he was at that razor's edge stage a man gets himself when he tries to show off with one orgasm more than the Good Lord intended in one day. He could still keep it up. But even when he started moving faster, he couldn't get himself over the edge. His legs were getting tired, too.

He said, "I got a better idea," and lifted her knees higher.

"Lock your legs about my waist so's we don't have to stop while I lift you some more."

She did as she was told, but as he pulled the rest of her erect against his body she giggled and asked what he had in mind. He picked her up off the table, still inside her, and moved around to sit in the hardwood chair with her in his lap, facing him. As she settled her pelvis deeper to absorb all he had to give her, Sine said, "Och, this feels bonny, too! Is there no end to your ingenuity?"

He saw that he might have made a tactical error when he tried moving his hips in this position. It worked better with small gals. Sine was a mite heavy to play bouncy-bouncy on his lap.

"Let me help, then," she said, and lowered her own bare feet to the floor on either side as she braced her legs and started moving up and down. "Och, this feels lovely!"

And she was right, although she moved too slow and teasingly for him as she slid up and down the full length of his excited but balky tool. He held her close, enjoying the way her nipples slid over his chest as he kissed her plump throat to encourage her. It did. She started moving faster until the chair was in trouble, too, as she literally tried to jerk him off with her whole heavy body. He decided the chair was on its own as he felt himself starting to get there at last. But then, just as he was sure he was fixing to let fly, the fool redhead stopped, groaning that she was coming again as she kissed him hard and ground her wet breasts against him. They were both sweating good by now. That didn't bother him. But she wasn't moving enough to finish him off, damn it!

He held her tight against him and rolled forward off the chair to do it right on the only surface handy, the rammed earth floor.

As they rutted on the dirt like wild critters, Sine protested, "I feel a *muc salach* down here on the naked soil. But, *Och mo mala,* I *love* it!"

She sure presented her love box at an interesting angle

121

with the hard dirt under her soft, well-padded butt. Long-arm's knees were hurt by the gritty floor, though, so he raised himself on stiff arms and legs to finish with some good old-fashioned long dicking, now that he was really inspired. She raised her head to stare down between them, giggling like a dirty little kid as she watched him sliding in and out of her red thatch. But it still wasn't working right. He was *sure* he could come with a dozen more strokes, but every time he counted a dozen, he hadn't.

She did, though, rolling her red hair uncaring across the dirt as she heaved and panted in orgasm. It wasn't fair. She'd *started* hard up.

Another position might help. He withdrew, rolled her over on her hands and knees, and quickly mounted her dog style before she could argue about it or he could go soft. Her back was gritty with dirt and her big rump was red from grinding on the same. The new view inspired him to greater effort as she gasped, arched her back, and said, "Yes, treat me like a wee beastie, you great insatiable stallion!"

Longarm was pretty sure he was licked. Like it or not, he had to stop sooner or later and he'd used up all his infernal ammo. He kept going. It didn't hurt, after all, but he knew the time was coming when he'd just have to pretend and tell her he was finished so they could part friendly before they both died of overwork. He grinned at himself as he studied what he was doing, wondering why he kept doing it. He knew that if this was Fiona or Nancy right now he'd stop willing enough. But, damn it, he'd screwed this redhead at least an hour and it didn't seem right to get up from the table without cashing in his chips at least one damned time.

She shoved her big pink rump higher, moaning that she was almost there again. He kept going to be polite until she pleaded that she couldn't stand another stroke and fell off him to roll across the floor, sobbing that she'd never come so often in one day in her entire life.

He said he was willing to forgive her for leaving the scene of the action as he got unsteadily to his feet and sat on the edge of the bed to recover his breath. His fool pecker was still standing up, like it hadn't just let him down. He knew he'd never forgive it, and some night alone in a sleeping bag, when it stood up lonesome, he meant to remind it they'd blown the chance to come in a perfectly presentable redhead.

As he relaxed, half-reclining on the bed with his feet on the floor, Sine rolled again to her hands and knees, looked about as if she wondered where she was, and crawled over to him, saying, "I think I died and went to heaven for a while. Och, thank you, Custis. You've no idea how much I needed that!"

Then she, too, became aware of his fool show-off erection and gasped with dismay, saying, "You can't be serious! I can't believe all that was ever in me—and, I'm sorry, but I'm starting to get sore down there."

He said, "That's all right, little darling. I told you I was a merciful cuss."

She crawled closer, raised her red head between his limp, widespread thighs, and took the matter in hand, saying, "Och, your poor thing. I fear I didna satisfy you. Though I fail to see how such a thing could be."

Then she kissed the tip, opened her moist rosebud lips, and proceeded to suck him off as Longarm stared in wonder at the bobbing part in her red hair for a spell, then lay back to close his eyes and take it. He'd been right about her mouth having an astounding capacity. The pretty little thing enjoyed having her mouth full. So he enjoyed it, too. Her skilled tongue and lips conspired to make him forget all he'd said about not being able to come again this afternoon. As she worked it even harder and bigger he knew he had at least one round in the chamber after all.

But as he felt himself starting to come at last, Longarm knew where it had to fire if all this work was not to count as an almost. So he sat up, reached down, and hauled her up on the bed, saying, "Let's finish right!" and, before the feeling could fade again, shoved it in her vagina without bothering to worry about positions.

She laughed as he entered her sideways, with her legs together and her knees raised as she lay on her left side. It wouldn't have worked had she been skinnier. But, thanks to her big hips, her important parts were high enough off the matress for him to finish in a frenzy of hard hot pounding as she sobbed, "You're killing me, you brute!"

She didn't mean it. She came, too, as he fired his delayed action into her, trying to kiss her right despite the odd position she was in. He settled for tonguing her ear as she giggled, arched her spine again, cried out aloud, and insisted, "God damn it, Custis, stop! Enough is enough—and didn't you say you had to ride into town?"

He tongued her ear again, rolled her over to kiss her right as he withdrew, and said wistfully, "Well, if you don't want to screw, now that we've gotten some preliminaries out of the way..."

"You daft loon," she giggled, "I won't be able to walk right for a week. How in heaven's name can you keep going like that? Never mind, I don't want to know. What time did you say that train was due in?"

He sighed, called her a sissy, and got off her. She rose to totter to the dry sink across the room and fetch them some clean rags to wipe themselves off with. As he started getting dressed, she stared at him pensively, hugging her naked knees up against her as she sat on the bed, looking like she wanted to say something.

He waited until he was strapping on his gun rig before he said, "All right, honey. Spit it out. What's eating you?"

"I feel so ashamed now that it's over. Do you think I'm a loose woman, Custis?"

"Hell, no, you're tight as a drum."

"Don't talk dirty. Not now. I know I threw myself at you. I know I behaved like a shameless slut. But you see, dear, a woman living alone gets so queer in her head and..."

He moved over to her, lifted her face with a gentle hand under her soft chin, and bent to kiss her tenderly, before

124

he said, "You didn't behave no worse than anyone else, Miss Sine. Don't go feeling guilty now that you've gotten some natural feelings under control again. What just happened was meant to happen, or the wind wouldn't have seen fit to blow your skirts up that way."

"I'm glad you didn't come in my mouth. I wanted you to, then, but now that I'm not feeling crazy . . . Och, Custis, I rutted on yon floor like a pig with a total stranger!"

"Shoot, I'm not a stranger. Not now. I'd say we know each other better than half the people we're ever likely to meet up with, social. I didn't think you was a pig when I was acting horny, Miss Sine. I'd be a liar if I said you didn't screw good. But you screw as ladylike as any lady I've ever screwed."

She laughed wildly. "Och, be on your way, you mad, gallant loon. Thanks to what happened I'll sleep well this night, though I'll never forgive myself. But . . . Custis . . . ?"

He said, "Yeah?" hoping she wasn't going to ask him what he didn't want any gal to ask him right now.

She licked her lips. "I know you're expecting to visit me again when you ride back this way, dear."

"That's true," he lied.

But she shook her head. "You mustn't. I'm sorry. I know I'll want you to, once I recover from what just took place between us. But we have to be strong. I know I just acted like a madwoman. But I've my reputation to consider, and—"

"I understand," he cut in, repressing a whoop of sheer relief as he made his face look sad and wistful. "You'll never know how it hurts to give you up forever, little darling. But you're right. We must be strong."

Then he kissed her and got the hell out of there before she could change her infernal mind.

Chapter 10

Longarm rode harder than he'd intended for Rabbit Wash after losing so much time with Sine MacTavish. He reined in now and again to see if anyone was trailing him, but he didn't see anyone and he hadn't really expected to. He made it to town before sundown, but it was still pretty dark. The storm clouds had come down from the Front Range to cancel the usual prairie sunset scheduled for that evening. As he reined in near the Western Union office a big fat frog, or what felt like a big fat frog, plopped smack on the flat crown of his Stetson. He dismounted, tethered Petunia to the hitching rail, and broke out his yellow oilcloth slicker as he told her, "I *said* it looked like rain. Just wait a few minutes and I'll see if we can get you under cover, too."

He went inside and asked the clerk if there were any messages from Denver for him. The telegraph clerk said there were none and added, "We haven't even sent your night letter yet, Deputy Long."

Longarm blinked. "Jesus, is it still the same day? Well, that just goes to show you how confused a gent can get when he's saddle sore."

"Been riding a lot today, huh?"

"You might say that, pard. I'll check back with you later."

He went outside again, chuckling to himself as he realized that, thanks to his active ways, old Billy Vail could still be wondering where the hell he was. Although, knowing old Billy, he'd probably figured it out some by now. But he wouldn't know for certain until he got that night letter. He pulled on the sticky, creaking yellow slicker and led Petunia toward the rail siding to see if they had a shed for her and any news of the Cheyenne train for him.

They had both. The old switchman said the train had pulled in less than twenty minutes before and that he'd enjoy Petunia's company if Longarm wanted to put her in the lean-to behind his combined quarters and signal house. Longarm asked the man if Silas Redford had gotten off the train. The old man spat and said he didn't know, adding, "I only switch 'em on or off the siding. I ain't no infernal porter!"

Longarm left Petunia in his cantankerous care and headed back the way he'd come. As he got his bearings better in the moody light, he saw that there was a lamp burning in the window of the *Custer County Clarion*.

He went in, called out, and Silas Redford stepped into view, frowning, then brightening to say, "Oh, it's you. I thank you for helping out poor Nancy this morning, Longarm. I just got in, and had she lain tied up here on the floor all day..."

"Who told you about it? That town law—what's his name?"

"I haven't spoken to anyone since I arrived. Nancy told me herself. She tracked me down in Cheyenne this afternoon to demand her back pay. I'll miss that girl. But, try as I might, I couldn't get her to come back with me this evening. She seems to think someone's gunning for us."

"What do you think, Redford?"

The newspaperman shrugged and replied, "What is there to think? It seems obvious some gents admired old Nancy. She ain't bad-looking with her glasses off. They tied her up in here just before you came in and then changed their minds about raping her. Then one of them went to her place, figuring she would be there alone—and, hell, you know the rest, Longarm. You were the one as shot the son of a bitch!"

"I shot another son of a bitch who followed me from town. Do you reckon he was out to defile my fair white body?"

Redford had to grin at the picture. He said, "There you go. Nancy said there were two of them. You seem to have shot them both. What makes you so mean, Longarm?"

"Wandering about in a state of total confusion, mostly. Nancy said she didn't recognize the one I shot in her hired room."

"Hell, son, she wouldn't have recongized you or me if she wasn't wearing her specs. Was she wearing her specs when she saw the prowler up in her place?"

"As a matter of fact she wasn't wearing any...ah, specs," Longarm replied thoughtfully. "I follow your drift. She said she didn't know him when all she could see was his boots. She was likely flusterpated."

"So she told me when we met up in Cheyenne. She didn't mention the second one you shot, since she couldn't have known. I, of course, know even less, since I just got here. I've been looking about to see if anything is missing or looks to have been trifled with. But everything seems in order. Like I said, they must have been ornery drifters bent on taking advantage of a not-too-bright but pretty gal left alone to watch the store."

Longarm said, "At least one fit the description of a hired

gun wanted in Dodge. His right-handed pinto-riding pard is still up for grabs, but, like I said, he wasn't trailing me with a buffalo gun to rape me."

Redford frowned. "Nancy told me she thought someone sent hired guns to keep us from printing something. I thought about it all the way down on the train. It don't work. I'll show you our next edition if you like. It's all set up back there, save for the last page, and that's nothing but advertising."

Longarm nodded. "I read this week's early edition. So did they, to hear Nancy tell it. I didn't see any news items worth a shooting, neither. Let's have a look at the advertisements you mean to run, Redford."

Redford looked surprised, but he shrugged and opened a drawer to haul out a sheaf of order blanks written in a feminine hand. He handed them over. "Help yourself. I wasn't figuring on starting to set 'em up until tomorrow or the next day. Wouldn't Nancy have noticed if we were running sinister advertising, seeing she wrote down the orders?"

Longarm spread the sheets on the counter as he observed, "You said yourself she was dumb. Let's see: I don't want to buy a sunflower windmill, used or brand new, at that price. I see you can buy agricultural machinery cheap enough here in cattle country. I know this brand of tobacco. Don't never smoke it unless you admire the smell of burning skunk. Damn, you're right as the rain outside. She never wrote word one about guns, dynamite, or antique Scotch daggers for sale."

He turned a page over. "Hello, what's this?" he said suddenly. "It's writ on both sides and that ain't the same handwriting."

Silas Redford took the sheet, studied it, and said, "Oh, I see what happened. Someone wrote an ad in my mail, and Nancy, being nearsighted, wrote that order for alfalfa pellets on the back, thinking she was using a blank sheet. Let's see, now, some gent in Custer County, Colorado wants to sell some mining machinery and a freight wagon, cheap. Name's Levine and he says you can contact him at the Pronghorn Saloon in Silver Cliff during business hours."

He handed the letter back to Longarm and added, "Must be a prank. Every now and again some fool tries to run an ad for left-handed shovels or rubber bobwire as won't hurt the cows. I don't recall anyone named Levine in these parts, and the address is phony, too."

Longarm scanned the letter again and said, "I was wondering who'd have mining machinery to sell up here, with the bedrock under at least a hundred feet of prairie loam. I take it there's no Pronghorn Saloon in said town of Silver Cliff, Custer County?"

"Hell, Longarm, there's no such *town* as Silver Cliff in this county. Look around outside, son. The nearest cliffs of any kind are mayhaps some sandstone hogbacks in the foothills to the west. Ain't one of them anything like a *silver* cliff. The *Custer County Clarion* would have printed it, had there ever been a mine of any kind in this neck of the woods."

Longarm pursed his lips as he ran his memory overtime. Then he nodded. "Silver Cliff rings a bell somewhere down a back alley in my head," he said thoughtfully. "I think I passed through a mining town called Silver Cliff a spell back. It was down near Pueblo, I think—and, yep, there *was* a saloon there called the Pronghorn. I remember 'cause there's a Pronghorn in Denver as doesn't charge so much for drinks, and serves better eats."

Redford shrugged. "There you go, then. Like I said, it's a prank. Some idjet tried to run an advertisement using an address he remembered from another time and place."

"Then what's the joke?" asked Longarm, staring morosely at the mystery letter. "I don't see nothing funny about a gent wanting to unload some old mining gear and a wagon, do you?"

"Hell, I never found left-handed shovels amusing, Longarm. Maybe it's a coded message. You know we don't run

131

anything dirty in the *Custer County Clarion*. But perverts wanting to set up something awful sometimes slip one by us by saying European art when they really mean dirty French postcards. Levine sounds sort of French, if you ask me."

Longarm said, "I don't think so. I know some Levines in Denver and they ain't. Matter of fact, they're mining men. Never mind hidden messages for now, Redford. How could you place an ad like this by mail order? How would the *Clarion* get paid?"

"By billing them by mail, of course. Nancy took care of that for me, damn her skittish nature. Naturally, if we'd run that, we'd have been stiffed if and when we sent the bill, since there's no such address in the county."

Longarm thought and asked, "Is your *Clarion* listed anywhere as a Custer County newspaper?"

"Sure it is. We're in the same directory of newspapers as the *Denver Post*. You don't want *my* address, do you?"

"Not hardly. I know where we are. Let's figure out where Levine is. Do you have a map of Colorado handy?"

"Hold on, I got an atlas back here somewhere."

Longarm managed to get a cheroot out from under his stiff yellow slicker and light up by the time Redford came back to place a big atlas on the counter between them. Longarm turned to the index, found Silver Cliff, Colorado, with its map coordinates, and turned to the page full of Colorado to trace it down. "Here we are. Like I said, just northwest of Pueblo and . . . What the *hell?*"

"Something wrong, Longarm?"

"More like loco than wrong. Look here at this map and tell me I ain't blind when I say that Silver Cliff, Colorado, is in *Custer County*."

Redford turned the atlas around to study it before he said, "By gum, that's what the map says, all right. But what's Custer County doing down *there* if it's up *here*, Longarm?"

Longarm ran his finger up the red line of the Burlington right of way until he came to Rabbit Wash, where they were standing. He swore and said, "This map don't say this part of Colorado is Custer County. This map says we're in *unincorporated federal territory!*"

Redford said, "That's loco, all right. Mayhaps this atlas is old and they hadn't incorporated the county when it was printed?"

Longarm shook his head. "That won't work, two ways. For one thing, it's agin the rules to have two counties with the same name in the same state. For another, this atlas was printed less'n three years ago. It wouldn't matter if it was older. There's a mess of Custer Counties in the West, most incorporated right after Little Bighorn, before the debunkers got to work on the poor gent's public image. The point is that this Custer County down near Pueblo got there first. Your county couldn't have incorporated as no Custer County. They wouldn't have let 'em, down at the Denver state house."

Redford looked completely bewildered as Longarm went on. "I see what this letter from Silver Cliff means now. This Levine who aims to sell some gear saw the name of your paper in the publisher's register. Seeing *Custer County Clarion,* he figured you was a local paper. Local to *him,* that is. He placed an ad by mail, addressing it to Rabbit Wash, like it ways on your masthead, and here she is. Right address, wrong county!"

Redford protested. "Wait a cotton-picking minute, Longarm! *All* my mail comes to Rabbit Wash, Custer County!"

"Well, sure it does. You can see the real Custer County's a bitty yellow blob on the map, easy enough to overlook, while Rabbit Wash at least sets on the Burlington line on the way to Cheyenne. The post office missed the double naming of counties. Hell, my office did, too, and I mean to have a good laugh on him when I tell him he ain't as good a paper herder as he lets on. Come to think on it, the Justice Department at least should have knowed, since they ordered us to investigate this here Custer County war. Let's see, now...Oh, I see. Someone sent word to Justice about the troubles in these parts, giving the names of the towns and saying it was Custer County. If they noticed that item about federal territory at all, they could have assumed like you that the map was out of date and that this was a new county. New counties is always springing up like mushrooms out here, so—"

"Hold on, damn it!" Redford cut in. "This *is* Custer County. It was Custer County when I got here to start my paper. Everybody in these parts *knows* they're in Custer County!"

Longarm shook his head. "You mean you all *think* you are. Who told you this was Custer County? Have you ever seen the county corporation papers, Redford?"

"Of course not. Does an immigrant ask to see the deed to the United States when he gets off the boat? Any county papers would be on file in the county courthouse over to Scots Wells, wouldn't you say?"

Longarm examined the glowing tip of his cheroot thoughtfully as he replied. "I would have said so until a few minutes ago. My boss was right. This case is a bucket of snakes. You know what we got here? We got us a mighty odd picture, if only I could fit it together. I was sent to find out who killed two sheriffs. Only now I find that neither MacTavish nor MacMillan ever *were* real sheriffs! I learned today the county was run sort of unconstitutional. Tonight I learn it ain't even a county! Some crazy old foreigners just went through what they thought was the motions when they set themselves up what the Scotch call a *duthas*. They selected county officials, Scotch style, and as the rest of you pilgrims wandered in, you were all told you were in Custer County and you never saw fit to question it. Come to think on it, I don't think I've ever seen the charter of the city of Denver or even West-by-God-Virginia, but I suspect they set things up more formal than here."

"That's no bet, Longarm. But if this ain't Custer County, Colorado, where in the hell are we?"

"I got to study on that. Got to send a mess of wires, too. But, off the top of my hat, I'd say that everyone in these parts is either squatting or homesteading on unincorporated federal range. You sure as hell ain't in Custer County!"

Redford shook his head as if he was trying to clear it. "Well, I always knew them Scotchmen were all loco. But what does this all *mean,* Longarm?" he asked.

Longarm said, "It gives me some motives for some otherwise just plain foolishness. Trouble is, now that I have me some motives, I have *too* many! I don't think either of the old chiefs know they've done anything irregular. Neither one's a lawyer and I've noticed they're living in a past when all a man needed to set up one of them clan duthas things was a bagpipe and some tough kids. But some of the younger, better-educated cusses could have figured they ought to make some changes. Neither Duncan the Grim nor Calum MacMillan are much for changes. So starting a clan feud might have struck someone as a good way to get one or both of the chiefs out of the way. It almost worked. Old Calum got shot in the head. Running off them political workers works the same way. Up to now, they've never held a proper election up here in whatever-you-want-to-call-it. Keeping folks from voting another four years figured to maintain the status quo until the stinkers could work things out more to their liking. Now all I have to do is cut the real villains out of a herd of just plain foolish foreigners. Like I said, a bucket of snakes."

Redford sighed. "It's beyond me, Longarm. What connection could all this business about county corporation papers have with those jaspers scaring Nancy this morning?"

Longarm pointed his chin at the letter from the right Custer County and said, "Easy. That's what they were looking for. Thanks to Nancy writing on the other side, they missed it. Someone found out an unfortunate ad had been sent to you for printing. They didn't want you to print it. They sent hired guns. Next question."

Redford said, "Jesus! I'm tempted to sell out and go print papers in some quiet place, like Tombstone or Dodge!"

"I can see why. Damn, I wish Nancy was here, now that

I got some sensible questions to ask her. Like who she might have told about that letter from Silver Cliff. Women talk to everyone, and it might have puzzled her some."

"It's puzzling me, and I'm still here!" Redford said. "Do you think I'd best not print anything you just told me, Longarm?"

"It's up to you. Do you feel like running the story?" Longarm asked.

"I do and I don't. It's hot news, for sure. On the other hand, I'm not a gunfighter!"

Longarm told him to do as he found fitting and stepped outside into the storm. He avoided the worse of the rain by hugging the buildings under the front awnings as he made his way back to the Western Union. He picked up the fixings and told the clerk, "This is your lucky night. I've got to wire all over creation. By the way, does Western Union think you're in Custer County?"

The clerk looked blank and said, "Well, sure they do. Matter of fact, each office has its own code number. Saves time to just wire a number instead of tapping out the whole address. Why?"

"I just figured out how the post office keeps screwing up, too. Mail sorters naturally send inter-city mail to numbered post offices. Did you ever hear about another Custer County, Colorado?"

The clerk started to shake his head. Then he brightened and said, "Come to study on her, I do remember a mix-up a while back. Some old coot said there was another Custer County somewheres. I told him there were Custer Counties all over, but that we'd get his wire through if he had the township and the street address right. Why?"

"Never mind. It's starting to sound tedious to me, too, and I got a mess of messages to send."

It was quite a few minutes before he handed the sheaf over. "May as well send all these night letters, too," he told the clerk. "None of them offices will be open at this hour. Bill 'em all to my Denver office."

The clerk said he would and added, "Oh, I almost forgot. We have a wire for you, too."

He handed it across the counter. Longarm tore it open and read it.

HAVE YOU GONE LOCO OR ARE YOU DRINKING AGAIN STOP EXPLAIN INSUBORDINATION AND EXPLAIN IT GOOD LEST UNDERSIGNED ARRIVE PERSONAL TO STOMP SOME SENSE INTO YOU YOU LOCO SUICIDAL WHIPPERSNAPPER STOP YOUR BOSS REPEAT BOSS

Longarm chuckled and put the wire away. The clerk asked if it was an important message. Longarm said, "Nope. My Uncle Billy just sends his love."

He went out again and stood in the dripping darkness to plan his next move. After the day he'd put in, his only sensible move would be to go back to Scots Wells and sleep a million years alone. On the other hand, it was raining like hell, and every once in a while the sky lit up and thunder boomed. This was no time to ride across the rolling prairie. He had no place to spend the night in Rabbit Wash, since old Nancy had lit out. He shuddered at the thought of spending a night with any woman right now, anyway. He headed for the town saloon, trying to stay out of the rain. With the wind gusting this way some rain always got in through the nooks and crannies of even a good slicker, and this one was due for retirement.

He saw the glow of the saloon ahead and walked faster as the rain pounded above him on the overhang. He was passing a slot between two frame storefronts when a voice behind him yelled, "Longarm! Duck!"

He didn't duck. He crabbed sideways into the slot, groping for his .44 and cursing as his hand got hung up in the sticky fold of oilcloth. A shot rang out in the night and something harder than any raindrop tore wet splinters from the corner he'd taken cover behind.

He got the .44 out at last, but since he was forted good he stayed put until the same voice called out, "Longarm? You all right?"

"I reckon. Who are you and what's up?"

"It's Wagner, the town law. What was up is down. I was tailing him as he was tailing you. When I saw him drawing on your back..."

"Say no more, pard," called Longarm, stepping out from cover but still keeping his .44 aimed until he spied the figure of the other lawman and a prone form on the wet walk between them.

Longarm was sorry now that he hadn't bothered to remember old Wagner's name. In truth, he hadn't taken him seriously enough to study on. But he didn't say so as they met above the downed gunman. Wagner rolled the man over with a boot and stared morosely down at the chalky face in the dim light. He said, "Yep. It's the same gent. But I still don't know who he was."

"How come you were tailing him, then?" Longarm asked.

"I just told you. I didn't know who he was. He's been asking all around town about a man he's looking for. I spotted him for a troublemaker. Now you know as much as me, Longarm."

"No, I don't. Was he asking about me?"

"Nope. Said he was looking for a gent riding a pinto and wearing a Spanish hat. Said the gent was to meet him here today. But, for such a small town, they couldn't both be in it at once. The barkeep at the saloon ahead pointed him out to me earlier. Nobody mentioned I was law, of course, and as you might have noticed, I don't stand out in a crowd. I didn't like his looks, as I said, and being I had nothing better to do, I've been trailing him. It's easy to trail a man in this storm."

"I just found that out. I remember a sort of Spanish-looking hat flying out of some grass earlier today, too. Let's

138

see if he's got any I.D. Did you see him talking to anybody since he left yon saloon?"

Wagner knelt on the wet planking to pat the dead man down. "I can't say as I did or didn't," he replied. "I was trailing him well back, and you can see how many slots and spooky shadows there are along Main Street after dark. He didn't talk to nobody noticeable. I lost sight of him for a spell when he stepped into a slot, probably to take a leak or something. That was when you came along, but you were too far off for me to call out to you. I would have, had I knowed he was after you. But to tell the truth I never recognized you in that slicker till you passed a lit window back there a piece. He must have recognized you, too. So when I saw him throw down on you I threw down on him, and here the bastard lies. Here's his wallet. Let's see. According to these papers, he's a private detective named J. Walter Johnson, from Arkansas. Ever heard of him, Longarm?"

Longarm nodded. "You just collected another reward, Wagner. The private bounty-hunting permit is long expired. He lost it by abusing the privileges as go with it about eighteen months ago. Since then he's been on the dodge, with some modest money posted on him, dead or whatever. He was a hired gun and wanted murderer, till just now."

"Hot damn! You mean I get to keep *this* one, too?"

"Well, sure you do, Wagner. *I* don't have any use for him, even stuffed. Let's get some old boys to help us with the body, and then I mean to buy you way more than one drink."

Wagner got to his feet. "I sure could use it. I ain't used to gunning gents. It's always been so peaceable around here. How come hired killers seem to be migrating like geese through Rabbit Wash these days, Longarm?"

"That's easy. Some son of a bitch has been sending out for help with his local chores."

"Have you any notion who's hired all these gunslicks, Longarm?"

139

"Nope. That part's more complicated. I'm going to have to study on catching one of the bastards alive. Up until now, I haven't been able to have a sensible conversation with one of 'em."

"Oh, did I do wrong, Longarm?" the town law asked.

Longarm held out his hand to shake, soberly, as he said, "Not hardly, pard. Had you missed the son of a bitch, I wouldn't be fit right now to hold a sensible conversation neither."

Chapter 11

The storm let up before midnight. So Longarm said adios
to his new pals at the saloon in Rabbit Wash, got aboard
Petunia, and rode her hard and sudden to get back to Scots
Wells before the sky changed her mind. The moon was
bright enough for Petunia to keep from running into anything
bigger than a bush and there weren't any bushes, so they
made record time.

He stabled the mare behind Fiona's place and rubbed her
dry before he left her to gossip with the other critters over
oats and water. But he didn't go right into the house. At
this hour everyone in town should have been bedded down
for the night. It was a good time to play burglar.

Longarm went to the county courthouse and picked the
lock. It would have been illegal even for a federal agent if

the courthouse had been legal, but at best it was bragging innocent.

He found the office of the sheriff's department, lit a table lamp, and rummaged about until he found a bunch of keys. He took the keys and put them in the side pocket of his coat under the slicker. As long as he was about it, he used the keys to let himself into other offices in the creaky old building. He was tempted to take some of the county records home to read in bed, but they were likely useless, and he was mighty tired. Since he had the keys, nothing was going anywhere for a spell in any case.

He locked up tight and went back to Fiona's. The pretty little gal was sitting in her kitchen in a robe, looking worried. He said, "Howdy, honey. I told you not to wait up for me."

She said, "I was sure ye'd never return, darling Custis."

He bent over to kiss her. "That makes waiting for me even dumber."

She laughed. "Och, ye're dripping all over me! Get out of those wet clothes while I prepare ye a midnight supper. What would ye like wi' yer tea, darling?"

"Anything but scones. Matter of fact, I ain't hungry enough to put you to the bother."

"Aye, I smelled more than one wee dram on yer breath just now. Do I have yer word ye were drinking half the night wi' yer own sex?"

He started peeling off the slicker as he grinned lewdly and replied, "Hell, I never drink with my pecker, girl. I drink with my mouth."

She frowned slightly and asked, "Was that an evasive answer, Custis?"

"Sure was. I'm ashamed to talk about more serious sinning since I got up here. So far I've only laid a blonde, a brunette, and a redhead. I usually do better. But, what the hell, I ain't seen a señorita or a China doll since I got off the train from Denver."

She called him a loon and got up, smiling, to rustle up a midnight snack of cheese and toast with tea. By the time she'd set the table Longarm was down to his shirtsleeves and damp pants. As they ate he asked if she had any reading material in the house. "I'm wore out from riding all over creation, but my head's still awake. I'd admire reading myself to sleep. It's another vice I don't want anyone to tell the Reverend Bell about. By the way, do you go to his church? He seems to think it's important."

She grimaced. "Och, that old snooper? Dinna frush yersel' about him. He preaches to more empty pews than filled ones. I can't attend Mass here in Scots Wells. We used to have a Papist priest when I was wee, but he died."

She shrugged and added, with a sad little smile, "Ye might have noticed I'm not very religious, anyway."

"Hold on. It's your own affair if you're a lapsed anything, but are you saying you're a lapsed Roman Catholic? I thought all you Scotch folk was Calvinists."

She shook her head and explained, "Only in the Lowlands. Highlanders held out for the true faith longer than the rest of Scotland, though by now most have become Protestants of one kind or another. It was hard to keep the faith in the glens after the final defeat of the clans at Culloden. The winners drove all the Papist priests to France wi' poor Prince Charlie, and—"

"No more ancient history!" he cut in. "Stick to the here and now in Scots Wells. I might have knowed from all the steeples I see growing here that things was complicated. But it's sort of interesting that you folk let your chiefs tell you who to get mad at, but don't say word one about your praying to the Lord."

She poured more tea for him as she explained. "The traditions of the clans are older than any kind of Christianity. When the clans were strong in the auld country it's true the wee folk were expected to follow the particular faith of their Toshach, even when and if he changed it. But over here, as ye've no doubt seen, the power of our elders is waning. As a matter of fact, most of us younger Scots who'd grown to adulthood on this side of the main ocean had almost forgotten the auld ways until this feud began."

He left the tea untasted, not wanting it to keep him awake, as he knew three strong cups might. He lit a smoke instead before he said, "Now, that's mighty interesting, Fiona. What you're saying is that this feudal clan war strengthens the hands of the old men who might have felt they was losing their grip. I've already read the Good Book. I don't suppose you'd have any reading matter on them clans of yourn? I can see that, tedious as it sounded in *Fair Maid of Perth*, I'm just going to have to bone up on the subject."

She shook her head and said, "No child raised Highland has any need to look such matters up in bookies, dear. We MacPhees didn't carry it to such extremes, but it's said the MacNeill Of Bara required his children to recite their clan genealogy before they were allowed to sit down to a meal. My father thought it enough that I could call the roll of allied Jacobite clans now and again."

She pursed her lips thoughtfully. "The Stuarts of Appin, of course, were related to the Ard Ri himself. Clan Donald was oft at war wi' the MacLeod, and in times of peace Clan Cameron fought Clan Chatten now and again. But when threatened by the Campbells and their Lowland allies, the Cameron of Lochiel and the MacIntosh of MacIntosh could forget past differences. Let's see—MacInnes was ever ready to stand for Gaeldome as was MacLean and Lamont, while the Sinclairs and Clan Mhorgan, alas, were wi' Campbell, along wi' Munro and—"

"Stop right there!" He laughed, explaining, "I ain't about to remember all them names, even if I wanted to. It's the system itself I'm interested in. Old Campbell mentioned a writer named Logan who, Campbell said, had it down in just one book. Ever heard of said book?"

"Nay, my father was not one for reading, I fear. Can we go to bed now?"

He managed, with an effort, not to groan. He smiled instead and said, "You know my mind pretty well, don't you, honey lamb? But you told me before, that you couldn't."

She said, "Well, to tell you the truth, I'm not the woman I was when first we met. I canna pleasure my ainsel, but if ye want me to . . . well . . . do some bawdy French tricks for ye . . ."

"Glory be, that sounds like more pleasure than I deserve!" he said. "But I dunno, Fiona. It don't seem fair, unless I could return the favor."

She laughed. "Och, I'd hardly expect you to! But I dinna mind putting ye properly to sleep, darling."

He pretended to be considering before he shook his head wistfully. "We'd best be strong, Fiona. I'll admit your words is giving me a hard-on, but I'd hate myself in the morning if I took such a one-sided advantage of you. We'd best wait until you're back in shape for us both to go at it hammer and tongs. By then we'll be so horny it'll be well worth waiting for."

She smiled radiantly at him. "Och, Custis, you dear man, ye're sae understanding. It's grand to ken ye have delicate feelings after all."

So she put him to bed. She even sat on the bed and watched by candlelight as he undressed. He was sort of worried about that as he shed his pants, but his show-off pecker, bless its little heart, was trying for a semi-erection. She sighed and said, "Och, ye've marvelous self-control, I see."

"You'd best leave us alone before it springs to full attention and I lose all sense of shame, little darling," he said.

She laughed, stood up, and kissed him good night with the bottom of her robe discreet but one nice little tit exposed to rub against his naked chest as he kissed her back with a heap more passion than he felt right now. As soon as he was alone, Longarm fell into the lavender-scented sheets, and fell sound asleep.

He was dreaming that someone was firing a bagpipe at him from a heather-covered rise while naked gals sat around him on toadstools offering to French him, as well as he understood their Gaelic.

145

Just as the dream was getting interesting, someone was shaking him by the shoulder and saying, "Custis, we have to get you up!"

He groaned, "All right, but you'll have to get on top until I'm wide awake, at least."

Fiona shook him again. "I'm serious, dear. There's going to be a *meeting!*"

He opened his eyes. The sunlight through the lace curtains said it was going on eight-thirty or even nine outside. He shook his head to clear it as he muttered, "Jesus Christ. I must be getting old to lie here slugabed halfways to noon! All right, honey, I'm up."

"Thank God. What are you to do about the meeting, dear?"

"Beats me. Am I invited?"

"No, thank God. The meeting will be between Gordie Thompson and Angus Bethune, man to man and weapons optional!"

He sat up, grimaced, and said, "Oh, *that* kind of meeting. Do you know when and where?"

"Aye, I just heard about it when I went out back to water the beasties. The MacRaes across the alley told me. The clan champions have agreed to meet in the middle of Main Street at high noon for a battle to the death!"

He rubbed a hand across his face. "I didn't suspicion either of them of having common sense," he mused. "They must have read some of Buntline's Wild West magazines of late. No sensible man would ever agree to such a fool notion. I can't come up with a better way to get killed than to announce to your enemies that you'll be at a particular time and place with no cover and good light. Is there any tea on the stove, doll? I got to get cracking and, damn, this throws my timetable off again!"

She said there was always a pot warming on her stove, so he got up and dressed without a bath or a shave to inhale some tea and wake up all the way. He felt sort of sweaty, but then he wasn't fixing to go to a dance at noon.

Getting out unseen was a problem at this late hour, but he licked it, or would have, had not the Reverend Bell met him near the mouth of the alley. The preacher pursed his already prim lips at the unexpected sight of Longarm and said, "Well, I hope ye have an explanation for this. What were ye doing in yon alley?"

"Taking a piss, sir. Have you any late word on the fool duel that's supposed to take place in a few hours?"

"I don't know what you're talking about. I demand to know where you spent the night. For I've asked all the decent folk in town, and nobody can tell me. Have you been sinning with a woman of the town, Deputy?"

"If I told you half of what I've been up to you'd faint dead away. I've got some more important snooping for you, Reverend. I'll drop by your church later. I want a list of any parishioners of yours who aint Scotch."

"I don't have any Sassenachs in my wee flock. But even if I did, I don't work for you. I'm engaged in the business of the Lord."

"Go peek in some windows, then. You've answered the only question I had for you, and I'm obliged. Now I got some business of the government to tend to, so adios."

He went down to the courthouse, unlocked the door, and went in to find some foolscap and a red wax pencil. He neatly lettered a sign: CLOSED UNTIL FURTHER NOTICE BY ORDER OF THE UNITED STATES GOVERNMENT. NO TRESPASS-ING. SURVIVORS WILL BE PERSECUTED! Then he rummaged out some thumbtacks, went out to post the sign on the front door, and locked the same again.

He moved down the entrance hall to the lockup and fumbled different keys into the lock until he found the right one. Inside he found a small guard room with a fairly stout-looking prefabricated cage against the back wall. He nodded in satisfaction, made sure nobody had left any weapons about since the last sheriff had vacated the premises via a pine box, and locked up again.

As he turned from the door a morose-looking gent dressed

for preaching or undertaking was standing nearby, regarding Longarm with considerable displeasure.

Longarm said, "Morning."

The old gent asked, "What is the meaning of the sign on yon door?"

Longarm smiled thinly. "Means just what it says, in plain American. I don't know how to write in Gaelic. Custer County just went out of business until further notice. I'm a U. S. federal deputy, as you must have heard over your backyard fence by now, so in the absence of any constitutional government, and being as all this foolishness squats on unincorporated federal territory, I'm taking over until Washington and the state of Colorado can work something sensible out."

"You must be mad, young man! We have our own county government here!"

"Not no more. I'm on my way to see old Calum next, and if he's still alive I mean to tell him he's not in the coroner business no more. Are you the parson of that handsome-looking Campbell church over there?"

"I am indeed! I am the Reverend Loudoun, and I defy ye to put *me* out of office!" the preacher cried.

Longarm chuckled and said, "I'd like to. Can't. The Constitution says anyone can run a church most any old way, as long as they refrain from human sacrifice, temple prostitution, and such. But you can do me a favor if you run across any Campbell men. Tell 'em to tell Duncan the Grim what I just done here."

"I will indeed! And if you have the brains of a gnat you'll be well away and riding hard by the time I do so!"

Longarm shook his head good-naturedly and moseyed off, hitching the cross-draw rig under his frock coat to ride his left hip better. He went next to Doc Essex's house and knocked on the door. The doc's wife answered. She said the doc was out birthing a baby and that old Calum had been sent home to the Double M and was expected to be up and about whenever he felt up to it. Longarm thanked

Mrs. Essex and went back to the main drag.

It was deserted, end to end. Fiona hadn't been the first or the only one to hear about the meeting. He looked at his watch and swore. He was spread too thin on time. He had to visit the Western Union in Rabbit Wash to read the answers to his night-letter questions. But there was no way in hell he could make it to the railroad town and back before noon.

He thought for a moment, nodded, and headed for the Thistlegorm Saloon, closest to the town and county offices he'd just taken over. He knew that if he had time to kill, a man who'd issued an invite to a walk-down might have risen early after a restless night, too.

The Thistlegorm was open, as early as it was, and when Longarm stepped inside he saw he'd been right about Angus Bethune. The big ramrod of the Double M was bellied up to the bar solo, drinking beer and whiskey for breakfast. The bartender had already thought to take down the mirrors and bottles behind the bar. When he saw Longarm looming in the doorway he must have decided to take a leak out back. He said something softly to Bethune and vanished from humen ken through a rear doorway.

Bethune scowled at Longarm and growled, "Are you looking for a drink or a fight, Longarm?"

Longarm said, "Neither. I've come to do my Christian duty."

Then he whipped out his .44 and laid it against the side of Bethune's thick skull, just hard enough to put him on the floor for a spell without damaging him permanently.

Bethune lay flat as a log on his face, not even groaning much, as Longarm squatted over him to unsnap the handcuffs from the back of his gun rig and cuff Bethune's wrists behind his back. Then he rose, picked up Bethune's beer schooner from the bar, and poured the contents over him, saying, "Rise and shine. Now that I've saved your fool ass, I'm taking you to jail for a spell."

Bethune gasped, sputtered, and said something dumb

about killing Longarm as soon as he felt better. Longarm hauled him to his feet, shook him like a willful child, and said, "We'll go out the back way and ease you down the alley to the lockup. I hate to make a grown man look foolish, even when he is a fool."

"Damn you, Longarm! You'll die for this!"

"You're repeating yourself, old son. Come on, out the back. Don't drag your fool feet or I'll lay you out again and drag you there."

He frog-marched Bethune out the back of the Thistlegorm and roughly swung him the right way, saying, "Keep moving. This would be a mighty inconvenient time for me to meet up with Clan Campbell, and the results could be fatal for *you!*"

"You son of a bitch! You hit me without warning!"

"Now, where in the U. S. Constitution do it say a peace officer has to give a formal warning to a disturber of the peace, Bethune? You poor blowhard cow waddie, did you really think you was a gunfighter? For God's sake, you let me walk right up to you and take you face to face without even gunning you, and you *said* you didn't *like* me!"

"Damn it, I wasn't braced for a shootout with *you,* you sneaky bastard!"

"I know. That's why I didn't divulge my plans in detail ahead of time. You see, son, real killers seldom tell a whole town who they're gunning for hours ahead of time. Hardly anybody would ever get killed if gents like John Wesley Hardin or Kid Antrim sent formal invitations to the dance. Hardin did send word to James Butler Hickock, one time. But old Hickock just forted up good in a whorehouse and sent back word that if Hardin was all that interested in a fight he could just come up the dark stairs with his back to the light and they'd work something out. Nothing much happened, since not even Hardin was crazy enough to stick his head in a bear's den occupied by Jim Hickock in a pensive mood."

They crossed a side street unobserved by anyone who

wanted to make anything out of it. The next and last block
was short, as Longarm recalled. He said, "Just keep walking, boy," and when Bethune protested that he was not a
boy, Longarm stiff-armed him to a faster pace and snorted,
"You're right. You're a damn fool *baby!* And now I mean
to put you in your crib where you can't get hurt. Jesus
Christ, drinking whiskey with beer chasers when planning
a premeditated shootout is too dumb for a tough three-year-
old to consider!"

"You talk mighty brave, considering I'm wearing handcuffs, you damned old Sassenach! You want to take 'em
off me and give me back my gun afore you calls me a baby
again?"

"Don't talk like an asshole. I already know you're one.
Can't you get it through your thick Scotch skull that when
you call a man your enemy he don't owe you *anything*, let
alone common courtesy?"

"Bah! *Real* men fight fair, damn your Sassenach ways!"

"Yonder's the lockup. Keep walking. Was you expecting
Gordie Thompson to fight as dumb as you?"

"Of course. He's a Scot, even if he is a Campbell,"
Bethune replied.

"I can see why Scotland's governed from London these
days, then. I know this comes as a shock to you, sonny,
but gents who take war as a serious business instead of a
sport generally *win!*"

"You had no right to interfere in the Highland gentle-
men's agreement between me and Gordie, damn it!"

The conversation was getting tedious, so Longarm didn't
answer. He unlocked the front door, shoved Bethune inside,
then locked him in the cage before he said, "Turn your back
to the bars and I'll take off the cuffs."

Bethune did so, growling, "You didn't even have the
nerve to free my bare hands where I could get at you, right?"

"You're learning, sonny. I'm a trained lawman, not a
professional wrestler. Just hold on and I'll see about some
food and water for you, later."

He went back outside. A small crowd had gathered in the square to stare and mutter at him as he walked across the grass toward them. But they parted like the Red Sea for Moses as he walked on toward the Argyle Arms.

Longarm didn't walk down the center of the deserted street as the sun rose almost directly above it. This was a real and somewhat tense situation, not a tale in one of Buntline's penny dreadfuls. He moved up on the walk on the Campbell side and hugged the buildings as he moved in the dark shadows of the shop-front awnings. It was a longer walk to the Argyle Arms than he'd remembered.

He came to a slot between two frame buildings and slid into it to go in the back door of the Campbells' saloon. It was well he'd done so, he saw, as he eased into the barroom and saw Gordie Thompson and Ian Mhor covering the front entrance from behind an overturned table, with their backs to him. The only other man in the place was the keeper behind the bar, who blanched when he saw Longarm. Longarm put a finger to his lips and sent him a silent message with eyes as friendly as twin gun muzzles. So the bartender kept quiet as he sank out of sight behind the thick mahogany.

Longarm moved in on the balls of his feet, silent as a cat.

Ian Mhor was whispering, "See anything, Gordie? MacIvor said the Sassenach was coming for sure!"

Gordie Thompson didn't get to answer. Kneeling as they were, their heads were at the level of Longarm's waist. So he just reached out and slammed their heads together hard.

It worked for Gordie Thompson. But Ian Mhor had fewer brains to bruise, so Longarm had to kick him in the head again before he had them both sleeping peacefully at his feet.

He turned and called, "You can come up for air now, bartender. I need some help getting these two boys to the lockup. Anyone can see they're both right sizable."

He heard no answer. The bartender had obviously crept along the back of the bar to go take a leak or run for help.

Longarm swore, cuffed the two unconscious men together, and stepped over to the window. Two riders were coming down the main street, looking confused and lost.

Longarm stepped out on the walk and called out, "Smiley, Dutch, over here!"

The two deputies spotted him, rode in, and dismounted. One of them said, "Don't get sore, Longarm. It was Marshal Vail as sent us. It wasn't our notion. Where the hell is everyone *at* in this town?"

"I got two prisoners inside. For once I ain't sorry to see you. Billy Vail done right for a change. I just noticed I only got two hands."

Chapter 12

Smiley and Dutch followed Longarm inside the Argyle Arms. Smiley had a name that didn't really fit him. He was a tall lean individual who looked like a breed and might have been. He hadn't smiled at anyone in living memory. The short, stocky deputy called Dutch had a Germanic name nobody could ever pronounce and few tried to. He was more cheerful looking than his dark companion. He liked to tell dirty jokes, and some of them were even funny. But, when crossed, old Dutch could act meaner than a gutshot wolverine.

Longarm explained the situation to the other federal men. Smiley reached his long arm across the bar, helped himself to a bottle, and uncorked it with his yellow teeth.

Dutch said, "Well, if we've took over the town, do you want us to carry these boys to the lockup for you, or just string 'em up, Longarm? Marshal Vail says you're in charge here, though he did say something about firing you after you got back to Denver."

Longarm looked out to see if there was a buckboard handy to commandeer. Then he saw the crowd coming up the street. "I'll tell you boys what," he said. "Cover me on foot as I do some showboating. Smiley, put away that infernal bottle. This is serious. Them two clan leaders I told you about is walking side by side. I *figured* a Scotchman was a scotchman, when push come to shove."

Smiley stuffed the bottle in the side pocket of his black coat with one hand as he drew his .44 with the other. Dutch left his own sidearm holstered. He enjoyed showing off his lightning draw.

Longarm reached down, grabbed an ankle in each hand, and proceeded to drag the two Campbell fighters outside. Their heads bumped some going down the wooden steps to the dusty street, but they were knocked out anyway, so how much could it have hurt them?

As Longarm proceeded toward the town square, dragging the two men behind him, Calum MacMillan, Duncan Campbell, and more recently combined clansmen that would be needed to lay a modest railroad formed a line across the street. Longarm stopped in speaking range to be polite and said, "Howdy, gents. That rain last night sure cleared the air nice, didn't it?"

The two Toshachs exchanged glances. Then Duncan the Grim snapped, "What are you doing with the ankles of those lads in your Sassenach hands, Longarm the Insane?"

"I'm dragging them to jail, of course," Longarm said. "Anyone can see they ain't in any shape to *walk* there. Let me introduce you to my associates, Smiley and Dutch. Did you read the sign I posted on the courthouse door?"

"We did indeed, and the Campbell's richt!" Calum MacMillan said. "Ye've gone oot of yer wee Sassenach mind! I strongly suggest the three of ye gi' us the keys and

156

ride oot of here while ye still can. For I am the lawful coroner of Custer County, and if my auld friend Duncan, here, is forced to kill ye all, it'll be my sad duty to record it as justifiable homicide!"

Longarm shook his head and said, "You ain't coroner no more. The only lawful public official hereabouts is the three of us. I'll be proud to explain it all to you later, but right now I got to get these poor boys out of the hot sun. So stand aside."

They didn't. Duncan the Grim said, "Let go of those lads' leggies, you daft loon! Do you think the three of you can take on Campbell *and* MacMillan?"

Longarm replied in a flat, no-nonsense tone, "You may be able to put three growed men down. But not before we takes at least a dozen of you with us. So stand aside or fill your fist, old man. We're coming through!"

They stood aside. Nobody said anything but Dutch, who muttered, "Hell, nobody *never* wants to fight with me no more!"

A few minutes later they had Gordie and Ian Mhor locked up with Angus. They were all coming too and mad as wet hens. Angus knelt on the cell floor by Gordie and helped him to a sitting position. "Jesus, you've a mighty bruised head, Gordie," he said to his former enemy. "What are we going to do about this meddlesome bastard?"

Gordie said, "Kill him together! The feud is off until we get rid of these infernal *strangers!*"

Longarm ordered Smiley to guard the prisoners as he stepped outside again to see what all the ruckus was about. Dutch tagged along. "Hey, Longarm, did you hear the one about this old prospector and his she-male burro?" he asked.

"Later," Longarm said as he surveyed the growing crowd from the steps. The older chiefs weren't there. They were likely making war plans in either the Thistlegorm or the Argyle Arms. But a self-appointed leader in the person of a large, bulksome cowhand stepped forward to call out, "I

157

am Ludovick Towart and I ride for the Double M and stand by Clan Millan. I offer to fight you man to man for the freedom of Bethune!"

Longarm smiled thinly down at him. "We don't do it that way in this country, Louie," he said. "But it don't seem fair to have us two Campbells and only one MacMillan clansman inside. Dutch, arrest that silly son of bitch."

Dutch said, "With pleasure," as he stepped down into the crowd, materialized a gun muzzle against Towart's gut, and went on pleasantly, "Inside, boy. Any of you other gents want to come with him as well? No? Then stand clear and keep them hands polite!"

Dutch marched the latest prisoner inside, asking him if he'd heard the one about the farmer's daughter and the Indian medicine man. Longarm waited until they were out of sight before he addressed the crowd again. "All right, we've room for plenty more inside, and you gents are squatting on property just reclaimed by the U. S. government. Anybody still here the next time I come out will be arrested for walking on the grass!"

He went back inside. Smiley was drinking from his stolen bottle. Dutch had all four prisoners under lock and key and was trying to get to the end of another joke as they yelled awful things at him in a mixture of English and Gaelic. Dutch turned to Longarm. "These boys sure are lacking in humor, Longarm. What do we do now?" he asked.

"Well, if they behave, one of you had best send out for bread and water later. I got to ride over to Rabbit Wash for a spell. Can you two hold the fort till I get back? Smiley, for God's sake..."

Dutch said, "Don't worry. He shoots better drunk than sober. That one bottle won't even make him smile. What do we say if them local hoorahs come asking about the unexpected political developments, Longarm?"

"Tell 'em that sign says it all until I make a few more arrests. I'll explain in more detail once I know what the hell I'm talking about."

Dutch chuckled. "I'm sure glad *you're* in command up here. No offense, but ain't we behaving a mite high-handed, even for town tamers?"

"They don't listen much to sweet reason. But it seems the one way you can get two Celts to stop fighting is to give 'em both a common enemy. So act as high-handed as you can without really killing anybody if you can help it."

"I follows your drift. When I worked for the Union Pacific as a guard I once made the mistake of trying to break up a fight betwixt two drunk Irish trackwalkers. You go on about your business, pard. Me and old Smiley knows how to make enemies."

Chapter 13

Longarm didn't aim to walk to Rabbit Wash. So he headed for Fiona's place to fetch Petunia. The pretty blue-eyed brunette was waiting for him at the alley entrance, holding Petunia and the pinto, saddled and ready, by the reins. Longarm smiled down at her. She didn't smile back. She said, "Here are yer beasties, sir. Ye'll find yer slicker and other things fra' the hoose is tied to the saddle in place."

He sobered. "You heard what happened, huh?" he asked.

"I did. The town is talking of nothing else. I fear I misjudged ye, the more fool I. When I woke ye to tell ye of the meeting, I thought ye'd do the *decent* thing and take the side of poor Angus Bethune."

"Honey, I never said I was your *clansman!*"

"Ay, I ken what ye were to me, and I'm not yer honey,

I'm a Jacobite clanswoman to the death, ye horrid Sassenach!"

He started to argue the point, wondered why he would want to do such a silly thing as that, and mutely took the reins to fork himself aboard the buckskin and ride. As she watched him ride out of her life, Fiona MacPhee wiped a tear from her cheek and firmly turned her back on the sight of him.

Longarm didn't look back. He left the pinto at the jail and rode into Rabbit Wash without incident. As he tethered Petunia in front of the telegraph office the town law, Wagner, joined him to say, "I sure am getting rich since I met up with you, Longarm. Mind if I tag along? Who are we after today?"

"Ain't sure yet," Longarm said. "Got to read up on it some."

Wagner followed him inside the office where, as Longarm had hoped, a mess of wires awaited him. He scanned them quickly, nodding and clucking approval from time to time. Then he put them aside. "Last night, as we was drinking the storm out, you said something about a school library?"

Wagner nodded. "Sure. Like I told you, Rabbit Wash is too small to have a regular library. But Miss Tillie, the schoolmarm, lends out books to folks. I'll be proud to show you the way."

Longarm said he'd be obliged. So, leaving Petunia where she was, they started walking. As they passed the *Custer County Clarion* a she-male voice called out, "Yoo-hoo, Custis! I'm back!"

They stopped and he turned to see blonde Nancy standing there, smiling flirty. "I can see you got over your fright, Miss Nancy," he said.

She sighed, "Actually, what happened was that I couldn't get as good a job in Cheyenne. Come in. We're resetting the paper, and Mr. Redford will want to thank you for the big news you gave him!"

He said he'd stop by later. Nancy sort of batted her nearsighted eyes as she said she'd be expecting him.

They went on. Wagner sighed and observed, "She's not a bad-looking little thing. I'm a single man, too. But she seems sort of hard to get to know."

Longarm didn't comment. It would only have made Wagner wistful to tell him the blonde had screwed him on their first meeting. Wagner wasn't exactly ugly, he was just one of those uninteresting-looking gents. Longarm had dismissed him as a nonentity on their first meeting, too. But the drab-looking small-towner had been a real lawman when it counted.

Longarm said, "Sooner or later there's going to have to be an election up here, now that we know the whole informal situation is going to have to be formally incorporated. How'd you like to stand for county sheriff?"

"I'd like it fine. But nobody ever seems to remember my name. I doubt I'd win."

"You got to stop hiding your light under a bushel basket, old son. The recent gunplay in these parts has given you at least a modest rep. I'm going to make you look even better. You know, of course, that since this county was never properly incorporated, that copper badge on your vest don't mean spit in the creek?"

"Oh, my God, are you saying I'm nobody at all?"

"Nope. I'm deputizing you, temporary, as a U. S. agent. I got the power and so you got the job. You'll play hell collecting enough per diem to matter, but it'll look better in the papers if you're on record as a federal agent as well as a shooter of more than one wanted outlaw."

"I thank you kindly, Longarm. For I follow your drift as to what a brag I can make, come election time. What do you figure that might be, if all we see about us is technically open federal range?"

Longarm shrugged and said, "Can't say. Depends on how smooth the lawful incorporation goes at the state house. It's no skin off Colorado's nose if things is done right up here for a change. If them old clan chiefs over to the would-be county seat works together, they could get the paperwork done in no time. If they won't, they can't, and most any outsider could come in here and file homestead claims on anything that ain't already filed federal. According to a wire I just got from Land Management, that ain't much. I mean to point all this out to them when I ride back to let them cooled-off rascals out of the lockup."

"That ought to cool the clan war down, some. Why are we going to the school, Longarm?"

"I told you. I got to catch up on my reading. Now that I've met the official leaders on both sides, it's obvious to me that neither old Calum nor Duncan the Grim wanted to have a war. Some sneaky son of a bitch tried to start one by putting that personally addressed dagger into MacTavish and then gunning MacMillan so's both clans would have something to brood on."

"You told me some of this last night in the saloon. You reckon it was a junior chief, like Thompson or old Angus?"

"Nope. Neither one of them has the smarts to be so sneaky. A man dumb enough to meet an enemy face to face at high noon in the middle of an infernal main street don't strike me as the kind who'd knife or shoot a man in the back in the dark. By the way, that gent on the pinto with the buffalo rifle was another wanted killer you may as well claim the reward on. Here, this wire come in this morning from Boulder. You'll see that the description fits and he stole the pinto from the last gent he gunned down there. I reckon you'll have to send the pinto back when you get around to it."

Wagner whistled as he scanned the want and put it in his pocket for future reference. He pointed his chin at a red frame building ahead and said, "Yonder's the schoolhouse."

As they strode closer, Longarm spotted the sign on the door. "What the hell? It's closed! Ain't this a school day?"

Wagner thought for a moment. "Damn, I forgot," he

said. "It's some fool President's birthday. The bank will be closed, too."

"I don't want to open a bank account. But I sure need that schoolmarm's help. You know where she lives?"

"Ain't sure. Around here somewheres. I'd have it in my directory at the office."

Wagner turned and loped off, eager to please, before Longarm could stop him. Longarm shrugged and went on to try knocking at the schoolhouse door. It was worth a try.

It worked. The door opened after a time and a mousy little brown-haired gal with a pencil stuck in her bun said, "I'm sorry, sir, we're closed today for the holiday."

Longarm flashed his badge. "I don't want to go back to school, ma'am. Can I have a word with you, even if it is a bank holiday?"

She seemed impressed by the badge, and told him to come right in, so he did. It came as no surprise that the school was full of desks and such. She led him down the aisle and through a door beside the blackboard to a little office with big book racks all around. She asked him how she could be of service.

"I understand you sometimes hire out books, ma'am," he replied.

She dimpled sort of pretty as she said, "Oh, we haven't enough books for a proper lending library, and I suppose I'm not supposed to do it. But, yes, I do loan books out to people I know. Did you have a particular volume in mind, sir? I suppose I can trust the U. S. government."

He chuckled. "Don't bet on it. But I sure would like to see a Scotch book by some gent named James Logan. I don't suppose you have a copy?"

She brightened. "Oh, I think we do! Let me see."

He expected her to stare up at the books all about. But she moved to her desk, opened a file drawer, and searched through the index cards in it before she said, "Yet, it's in the next room."

She led him into yet another room full of bookshelves and a leather-covered chesterfield sofa. She sat him down and slid a stepladder along the racks until she came to the right place. Then she climbed up, giving him a peek at her not-bad ankles below the hem of her polka dot blue summer skirts, and hauled a big leather-bound tome from a top shelf. He rose to help by steadying her as she tottered down the ladder with the heavy volume. She had about a twenty-two inch waist, natural. Wearing that corset she measured more like eighteen inches if his hands were any good at rule-of-thumb these days.

She thanked him with a blush and it seemed only natural when they sat side by side on the chesterfield as he opened the big book and whistled.

"Lord have mercy, it would take me hours to go through all these infernal clans," Longarm said.

"I don't mind. As you see, school's out today."

He grinned and opened to the index as she asked just what he was looking for.

"Well, even with pleasant company, reading all the deadly doings of tribes I can't hardly pronounce could take more time than I have, even if I was interested," Longarm said. "I'll take it on faith that once upon a time someone did something awful at Glencoe. Here's what I'm looking for, for openers."

She leaned closer to follow his moving finger. Her perfume smelled nice as she asked, "Septs? What are septs, Deputy Long?"

"Call me Custis. A sept is a branch of a clan. Lots of Scotch family names are junior branches of some famous and doubtless unruly clan. Ain't it funny how many names I never would have took for foreign are really Scotch? Look here: there's Harris, Lewis, Lamont, Harrison, Nicholson, Taylor, Turner—and, yep, Vail. Ain't that something?"

"My name's Tillie Baldwin. Is that Scotch?"

"Let's see. I'll start at the top again. Here's Brown and Bowie. I never knowed Jim Bowie was a Scotchman.

Though, now that I study on it, I should have guessed. The Lincoln County War make more sense when you consider Chishom, MacSween and Bonney are Scotch names. The Texas cattle industry was started by Captain Ewen Cameron, who stole the first longhorns from the Mexicans. I reckon old habits are hard to break."

He started idly leafing through the pages, looking at pictures of folks dressed up in fancy checkered duds. Tillie pointed to a Scotch lady and said, "Oh, that's an attractive outfit, don't you think?"

"Bit gaudy for out here, ma'am. Tell me something. Do you recall who you might have lent this book out to within the year?"

"Heavens! Have you any idea how many people borrow volumes from us?"

He turned to the flyleaf and saw a sheet of stiff paper with the school's address printed on it. "You stamp each book when you hire it out, I see. What do these numbers mean?" Longarm asked.

"The date I loaned the book, of course. I have a ten-day limit. You'll note I don't have a rubber date stamp. But the numbers in red pencil show the date it was loaned and the blue numbers show when it was returned."

He counted mentally as he went over the dates. "Here's a place where they held the book over a month," he remarked.

She leaned even closer as she replied. "Is there? Oh, well, we got the book back, after all."

She was jammed against his shoulder awkwardly. So he put his arm around behind her to keep *her* from feeling awkward as he said, "You sure are easygoing next to the Denver Public Library, Miss Tillie. Do you make folks pay a fine if they bring the books back late?"

"Heavens, no. I run a school here, not a real library. I note the date, as you see, but what can I do if they bring them back late, save to chide them and, if they keep doing it, refuse to lend them another?"

167

"That sounds fair. You wouldn't remember who it was as kept this book out so long last winter, would you, Miss Tillie?"

"I'm trying to think. It's not easy to think about books with your arm around my waist...ah...Custis."

"I ain't being forward, just neighborly. It's important that I find out who borrowed this book long enough to study it a lot more serious than most folks would study a book I see now is mostly pretty pictures. You would remember if it was one of them Scotch folk over to Scots Wells, right?"

"I'm sure it couldn't have been. Nobody from out of town has ever asked to borrow a book from our school library, Custis."

He smiled and absently gave her a little hug as he said, "You've no idea how good that news is, Tillie. I reckon they told me true when they said real clansfolk had no need of books to keep tracks of all this blood and slaughter. But an *outsider* would, if he or she meant to stir up trouble betwixt paid-up clan members. Get a Mac or a Glen wrong and all bets would be off. I've been listening to it a spell, and I know I would have a chore convincing anyone *I* was a killer clansman without doing some homework."

She was breathing kind of funny. "Am I holding you too tight?" he asked. She fluttered her lashes and replied, "Too tight indeed for a lonely spinster who doesn't get company much. You're making me feel all flustered. Are you making advances to me, Custis?"

She hadn't said she wanted him not to, so he said, "Yep," reeled her in, and kissed her good.

He meant it brotherly, for he didn't aim to stay long enough to get serious. But she took his friendly kiss serious indeed from the way she proceeded with her tongue and slid one hand under the book in his lap.

He closed the book and moved it aside to get a better grip on her as well. They couldn't talk much with her kissing him so passionate and likely lonely, so they just made friends without speaking about it. It wasn't until he had her skirts around her waist and was putting it in her aboard the chesterfield that she same up for air and protested, "Oh, I couldn't! I hardly know you!"

Then she closed her eyes and crooned, "Oh, I guess I do know you, and it's hard indeed! But I wouldn't want you to think I did this with just any man, darling!"

He started moving in her teasingly as he grinned down at her and soothed, "I don't do this with just any woman, neither. Only the pretty ones."

She laughed like a mean little kid. "My God, would you call this a seduction? I've never quite known the difference between rape and seduction. Is there any?"

"Sure. Salesmanship. If you likes what I'm doing, consider yourself seduced."

"Oh, I do, I do—but is this proper?"

"Not hardly. To do it proper, we ought to take our clothes off."

She laughed despite the way she was blushing and said, "I could never undress in broad daylight, Custis. Ah, could you move a little faster?"

He did, and after he'd made her come she still couldn't take her duds off in broad daylight, but didn't object when *he* undressed her, save for the corset and high silk stockings above her high-button shoes.

She said she was too embarrassed to watch as he shucked his own duds. So he said to close her eyes and she did, and held them shut until he remounted her, naked and not yet satisfied, thanks to the luck he'd had the day before. She moaned in pleasure and rubbed her surprising breasts against his chest as he scraped his belly on her corset. Her stockings felt interesting locked around his waist, too. It made the sweet moist naked parts he was enjoying feel even nakeder. She came ahead of him, protesting she'd never be able to look him in the face again, then raised her head to peek and gasped, "Oh, my God, we look like a French postcard!"

He swung her around on the padded leather to kneel on the rug with her silk-clad thighs spread wide and her back propped up so she faced him as he proceeded to long dick her with a hand on each of her pert breasts. "Take a look and see if this ain't even more artistic, little darling."

She did, and closed her eyes, protesting, "Oh, this is so grotesque! One minute I'm sitting at my desk correcting tests and the next I'm posing on the rug! How on earth did this happen, darling?"

"I reckon correcting tests had you sort of bored, honey lamb. Ain't this more fun?"

"Oh, shut up and *do* it! I'm coming!"

He did, too, and felt it down in his insteps on the carpeting. For his old ring-dang-do was back in action, but as surprised as Miss Tillie to find itself where it was.

She giggled and said, "I felt that. I feel so queer. I can't seem to get enough, but I'm so embarrassed!"

There was a distant sound of knocking. She stiffened. "Who could that be? Oh my God!"

He said, "It's just my sidekick looking for me. If we don't answer, he'll go away."

"This is terrible! I feel so confused. Oh, my God, I'm looking at you and you're looking at me, and we're both naked and worse!"

He withdrew, rolled her over so her own knees were on the floor as her naked topside rested on the padding, then entered her from behind, saying, "There you go. Now you can screw all you like without having to regard my ugly features. I'm sorry I didn't shave this morning. I wasn't expecting to be doing this right now."

"Good grief! Do you think *I* was? Nobody would ever believe this! A schoolmarm is supposed to lead a quiet life!"

"Yeah. Ain't it boring as hell?"

She giggled and arched her spine to thrust her pretty rump up to him as she said, "Bore me deeper, please. I do feel less shame now. But, actually, I find you quite attractive, as well you should know by now."

"You're pretty as a picture, too, Miss Tillie."

She laughed wildly. "I can imagine the picture I'm presenting to you right now."

She moaned, pushed against him to take it all, and gasped, "Oh, that feels heavenly!"

So he came, too, as she contracted hard and milked him soft with her quivering love box.

He withdrew slowly. Tillie rolled atop the chesterfield and lay sobbing. He couldn't tell if it was from pain or pleasure. He sat beside her and ran a soothing hand over her soft heaving body, saying, "We'd best slow down for our second wind, little darling. Do you smoke?"

"No. Good grief!"

He reached down for his shirt on the floor with his free hand and got a cheroot and a match as she stammered, "About us...ah...meeting like this, Custis. I honestly don't know what came over me. I've read about things like this in books. Oh, if you knew how often I've only *read* about things in books..."

"Don't bust the spell by trying to explain purely natural events, honey," he cut in, rubbing her more personally as he smoked. "Sometimes reading romantic novels ain't enough. I know how it feels to be lonely in a bed built for two, honey."

She sighed. "Are no secrets safe from you?"

He laughed and replied, "Nope. I'm a trained investigator."

"You horrid thing! I thought we just met! Do you go about peeping in unmarried ladies' windows at night?"

"Don't have to."

She laughed sort of crazy, leaped up, and ran over to the bookcases again to go back up the ladder, presenting a much more interesting rear view this time as she got down a book in a plain brown wrapper. She brought it back to the chesterfield, blushing beet-red but grinning like they were kids swiping apples as she sat down beside him in her corset and stockings to open the book across their naked laps. "You're

171

right about reading stuff like this alone unsettling one. According to this book, what the people in the illustrations are doing isn't natural at all, but doesn't it look...well... *interesting?*"

He laughed and said, "I've seen this afore, honey. It's a dirty picture book, disguised as a warning by learned doctors to keep the publisher out of jail. You poor little thing. Have you been reading yourself to sleep at night with *this* sort of literature? It's no wonder you're so horny."

"I'm not the one who's horny, you brute! You came to look at a library book and the next thing I knew you'd ripped my clothes off me!" Then she giggled. "Look at what that big buck's doing to that young girl. Isn't it awful?"

"She seems to be enjoying it, from the way she's smiling."

"I know. That's what made me so curious. I...ah...was engaged a few times. But, heavens, none of my swains ever suggested any of *these* positions!"

He took a drag on his cheroot and observed, "Well, some gents are just born stupid," as she kept turning pages to show some pictures that almost shocked Longarm, though he tried to keep a live-and-let-live attitude.

She found a picture of what was at least male and female human beings, once you got their parts sorted out, and asked if he'd ever tried it that way. He said, "Too complicated. They was showing off in front of the doc, most likely. Let's make up our own acrobatics. Come on."

He got up, pulled her to her feet, and led her to the stepladder. In the end, of course, they wound up back on the chesterfield, doing it right. She'd gotten used to his naked company now, so she could tell him pard-to-pard that she thought she might have thrown her back out on that ladder. He agreed they'd gotten past pure pleasure into showing off and suggested they quit for a spell. But after they'd snuggled just friendly for a while, he remembered what he'd come in here for and said, "About that mysterious long loan of Logan's book. What if some ornery cuss borrowed a book and never brought it back at all?"

She said, sleepy-eyed, "Oh, I'd be able to track them down. When I lend out a book I write down the name of the borrower as well as the number and title of the book."

He grinned and said, "That's more like it! Would you have the name of the person or persons unknown who borrowed Logan's clan histories at the right time and long enough to find an old Scotch dirk in a hock shop and mayhaps copy that old Clan Donald curse?"

She got up, heavy-lidded, to go and get her notebooks from the other room. He called after her, "By the by, would you have a Gaelic dictionary?"

She came back in with a couple of notebooks and said, "Of course not. Who on earth would ever read them?"

"Yeah, you're right. A Scot who talked Gaelic wouldn't need one, and nobody else would want to wade through that God-awful spelling. The man I want used Logan's book and just picked up a word here and there in old Logan's English clan history. It's sprinkled throughout with words like duthas, sennachie, and such. Let me see it again while you go over your notes."

He turned to the first Mac to find MacDonald and started to dismiss the MacAlpin clan. Then he stopped and muttered, "Jackpot!"

"Find what you were looking for, dear?"

"Yeah, right out of the top of the Mac box! *Cumrick bas Alpin*. Logan says that means Remember the death of Alpin, whoever in hell *he* was. Let's see, here's some stuff about the MacDonald clan, and the Gaelic words are in italics. How are you doing with *your* research, honey?"

"I'm looking, I'm looking, you brute! First you come in here and ravage me and now you want me to read to you?"

Longarm skimmed swiftly through Logan's long section about the awful things the MacDonalds had done or had had done to them. Then he found it. He said, "Not a word about *cumricking* anything, but here's the antique spelling of Glencoe, CHLINNE COMHANN! Yep, I could doctor a dagger now to read Cumrick Ghlinne Comhann like an ancient Celt and I don't even have to pronounce it! Anyone with this book, a neat hand, and some blue vitriol could etch old pawn-shop Highland dirks. Now if only we had a library card for the son of a bitch we'd be in business!"

Tillie shook her head and sighed. "It's no use, darling. These notes were only meant for myself and never meant to be official library records. I thought I might have noted down who'd kept that book so long. But I must not have noticed it was overdue when they brought it back. I can't find anything!"

"I've noticed you can be impulsive," he said. "That's a looseleaf notebook. Any chance you could have lost a page or more?"

"That could well be the case, dear. You can see some of the ring holes are worn and the pages aren't numbered. Oh, dear, I so wanted to help you. What are we to do now, darling?"

He took the notebook from her, tossed it aside, and pulled her naked flesh against his as he said, "We've already done it, and it helped a lot." Then he kissed her.

She kissed back, albeit weakly, and said, "Could we hold that thought for later tonight, darling? I confess the real things wears one out more than just wishing and strumming. I *am* going to see you again tonight, right?"

"Don't hold me to a timetable, little darling. I'll get back to you if and when, and we'll try some more positions if and when. Right now I got to go catch me a skunk."

"But you said my records were useless to you, dear. Oh, if only I could *remember* who borrowed that silly book that time!"

"Don't worry about it no more," he said. "You got tests to correct if you want to strain your little brain. I want you to do one last thing for me, Tillie."

"I suppose I can, if it doesn't hurt."

"Later. This ain't your regular address, and anyone can see the schoolhouse is closed. I want you to keep things that way for the next few hours. You stay locked up in here where you can't get hurt. Don't answer the door to nobody but me. I'll knock like this."

He showed her the signal by patting her rump fondly before they both got dressed and parted friends.

Chapter 14

Wagner must have been hunting high and low for Longarm. He caught up with him on the short main street near the tracks and asked, "Where in the hell have you been? I thought you rid out, until I saw your mare was still here."

Longarm said, "I've been asking questions. I aim to ask more. If you tag along, don't run off on me like that again. I like witnesses when I question folks. Though, come to think on it, you're forgiven, Deputy."

"Where are we going now?"

"May as well start at the *Clarion*. They're expecting us."

He was right. Nancy glowed at him from behind the counter as he came in with Wagner in tow. He rested both hands and elbows on the counter. "Well, here I am, and I think I've got another story for you. Boss in?"

Silas Redford came into view, smiling. "He sure is, and

thanks to you, our circulation figures ought to go through the roof after the next edition comes out!"

"You're running the story about the county being improperly organized?"

"Have to. I know I'm going to annoy hell out of a lot of people, but it's too big a story to sit on."

"Yeah. By the time you print it most everyone will know, anyways. I'm riding over to the so-called county seat this evening to see how they want to works things out."

Redford frowned thoughtfully and asked, "Can they, at this late date? I thought with that feud going on and those old Scotchmen on record as childish lunatics who didn't even know they had to incorporate their settlement before they announced it was the county seat, the natural thing for the state government to do would be to—"

"Move the county seat here to Rabbit Wash," Longarm cut in. "It sounds sensible. Even if they started holding elections legal in these parts, with the clans at feud, one-half of the Scotch majority would be bound by Druid custom or something always to vote in a solid block against the other. So the *sensible* folk here in Rabbit Wash would swing every election with their minority but telling vote. Right?"

"Of course. That's why my editorial is in fact demanding Rabbit Wash as the new, or I should say first, county seat. We'll naturally have to come up with a new county name, since the old one's taken."

Longarm smiled thinly. "How about Redford County? You'd like that, wouldn't you?"

"That's hardly proper for me to say, is it?" Redford said.

"How come you're being so modest, Redford? Ain't you been pulling all the strings to make things turn out that way? Seems to me a man who aims to run a county ought to post the management's name on the property."

Redford lowered his gaze to Longarm's loosely cupped fists on the counter between them. His voice was coldly correct as he said, "I don't like the turn this conversation is taking, Longarm. Are you accusing me of something?"

Longarm spoke, just as coldly. "Not accusing, saying. I just come from the school library, and according to the records of Miss Tillie Baldwin you sure take an interest in Gaelic, for a sassy knack."

Redford went for the gun he said he didn't carry. He didn't make it.

The derringer cupped in Longarm's big right fist invisibly until then fired two rounds of .44 into the treacherous newspaperman before he could get the whore pistol out of his hip pocket.

Then all hell broke loose.

Longarm had naturally slid sideways along the counter as he fired. As Redford went down wearing a glazed expression and two red blossoms of blood on his shirtfront, a taller gent came out from behind the presses throwing lead.

Longarm had already left the empty derringer on the counter to go for his serious sidearm. As the professional Redford had been plotting with in the back put two rounds through the cloud of gunsmoke where Longarm no longer was, Longarm put three into him before he hit the floor.

As the second man went down, he got off a wild round that came nowhere near Longarm but ended with a dull thud and a scream in Nancy, down at the far end on their side of the counter. Longarm glanced to his left for the town law, but Wagner wasn't there.

Longarm muttered, "Might have known!" Then he heard the muffled sound of two more shots, from somewhere out back behind the building. Longarm vaulted the counter and ran the length of the shop to the open back door. He peered out cautiously. Another total stranger in trail duds lay face down on the dust near two tethered ponies. Wagner was standing over him with a smoking gun. When the town law saw Longarm, he nodded. "Last time I made my rounds I noticed two strange horses waiting for someone back here."

Longarm smiled. "You count good, don't you? I never saw the one who tried to get out the quiet way. I owe you again, Wagner. You *do* deserve to be sheriff here!"

Wagner came to join him, holstering his gun. "Well, you're pretty good, too," he said. "Digging up them library records was mighty slick. But once he knew you had, I reckon he had no other choice than to do what he done, the poor idjet."

Longarm said, "I was hoping he'd do what he done. For in truth I didn't have beans on them if they'd been smart enough to tough it through. Come on, let's see what we can get out of Nancy. She's on the floor with a round in her behind, but she'll live, and I hope she can fill in some details."

Wagner's jaw dropped and he stared like a spooked colt before he recovered enough to ask, "What are you talking about? I was right there when you said the library records showed . . . What *did* them library records show, Longarm?"

"Nothing. Miss Tillie needs help with her bookkeeping. Wouldn't have meant much in court if she *had* been able to testify that Silas Redford once borrowed a book. But men with a guilty conscience can be bluffed into acting foolish at times, as you just saw."

"Hot damn! The whole act was a bluff?"

"Yep, but don't let on to Miss Nancy till we slicker *her* some more, too!"

He led his bemused deputy up front to where the two dead men and the wounded Nancy lay in various stages of disrepair. Nancy moaned. "Oh, Custis, get me a doctor. I'm wounded mortal."

He picked up his derringer to reload it and put it away until he needed it to slicker someone again. He told Nancy, "You ain't wounded mortal. You're just shot in the butt, you murderous little bitch."

She sobbed, "Darling, how can you say that? Damn it, I'm a *victim!* You were both there when Silas drew on you and that other man shot me!"

Longarm sighed. "All right, if we're still playing games, I'll spell it out for both of you. Keep track of this questioning, Wagner. You'd best be the arresting officer, since she's sure to try to compromise me in court by saying I laid her now and again."

"Hot damn, Longarm, did you? How was it?"

"Fair to middling, Wagner, fair to middling. Redford, there, sent his lover girl after me to set me up for a killing. They'd tried to get me alone on the prairie already, but found out I was a tough target at any distance. So when they saw me in town, lady love here was left for me to sort of rescue and of course do what the gallant dumb knight is generally known to do to the damsel in distress."

"You mean take her home and fuck her fondly?"

"Careful with your lingo, old son. Ladies present. By the way, go around and lock the door before you pull the shade to show we don't want no other ladies in here just yet."

As Wagner moved to close up shop, Longarm went on, smiling down at the wounded blonde. "It was complimentary as hell of you to keep me so long in bed when all Silas told you to do was to get me stripped down and disarmed. But, what the hell, I was enjoying it, too, and it's amusing to consider that hired gun in your closet, likely jerking off as he waited to get the drop on me. We know that it didn't work. Old Silas, of course, had run up to Cheyenne to establish an alibi. You spooked without instructions and went after him. You met up there—by accident, of course, Cheyenne being such a tiny crossroads village. He come back to work things out another way while you stayed long enough to wire for more hired guns and then returned to get back in the game with that story about not being able to find a job after looking high and low for mayhaps all of a working day. You want more?"

"Custis, I don't know what you're talking about. What made you take *us* for your enemies? It was those crazy *clansmen* who killed people!"

He looked at Wagner and said, "She wants more. All right. In the first place, and the first thing I noticed, I kept riding back and forth from Rabbit Wash to Scots Wells.

181

Usually telling someone in either town I was leaving, but not when I was coming back, since I never knew myself. Leaving out the fact that the two of us just gunned two obvious hired guns your late boss was talking to in the back just now, every time someone tried to ambush me out in the grass, it was *leaving Rabbit Wash*. Never the other way around. So it didn't matter how mean them Scotchmen in Scots Wells cussed me. They never tried to *get* me!"

He turned to Wagner. "You want it narrowed finer, Deputy? Remember the other night when you shot that rascal off my back? I was wearing a yellow slicker nobody had ever seen me with, in the dark, where *you* didn't even recognize me until I passed a light. Yet that man I'd never met before was following me as you followed him."

Wagner said, "Hot damn! It was right after you'd talked to that rascal on the floor there, too!"

"Yep, and nobody else in town, save for one switchman and the Western Union clerk, who won't work as a suspects, since they had nothing to gain no matter who ran the county."

"I see how they worked it. The gunslick was looking for his pard, the one you shot off that pinto. Remember that moment in time I lost sight of him in a slit?"

"Sure I do. Redford, there, was who he was with. But screw every loose end. Suffice it to say that all the other suspects have been tested and found wanting. The two old war chiefs never even wanted a war in the first place. Their tough clan champions were just dumb but honest cowhands, tough enough as town bullies but not worth spit in a real killing matter. Speaking of which, I have to get back and turn them loose. Have you been paying attention, Nancy?"

"I'm bleeding to death, you bastard!"

"We'll get you a doc in a minute. First I need some confessing. I reckon we got most of the real killers. But whether you get off with a year or so in the pen or hang by your pretty neck depends on how helpsome a state's witness you want to be. You know, of course, that a handwriting expert figures to identify your feminine hand on that murder weapon your gang put in Sheriff MacTavish. What did you and Redford do, dip the blade in wax resist, have you neatly letter the saying through the wax with a dry pen, then dunk it in acid? The hardware down the street will be able to say if you bought acid about the time the library says you checked out that Scotch book to copy from, you know."

"I swear I never did that, Custis darling. It was Silas who lettered that old knife. I told him he'd get caught. I told him they'd never get away with it."

He shrugged and said, "I'm tempted to take your word, seeing as we're old pals, Nancy. But if you want me to say your handwriting don't match, you'd best tell us who them *they* is. Did your land-speculating backers in Cheyenne know how far Redford was ready to go, or did he just have a contract to deliver a disorganized mess for them to move in on?"

She reclined on one elbow, rubbing her wounded rump, and eyed the nearby corpse of Silas Redford with singular hostility as she said, "He wasn't paid to kill anyone, the fool! The deal was to swing public opinion with his newspaper. But hardly anybody ever bought the fool paper and so he started sending for men he'd met in his wanderings as a gypsy printer and...Damn it, Custis, my ass really *hurts!*"

"No more than mine would have, you murderous little darling. All right—the backers have lost money and that ought to larn 'em enough, if they weren't in on the killing. Just one more thing, to wrap it up neat. We got us a superabundance of dead killers who could have stabbed MacTavish and shot MacMillan. Who did what to whom?"

She paled. "That killer from Dodge shot MacMillan. I heard them talking about it."

"That works. He almost got *me* in the back. MacTavish was stabbed long before. I'd say before Redford saw he was getting in too deep to work without professionals and *sent* for some. MacTavish was a happy-go-lucky drunk. He was killed reeling home from a drinking spree. But a total stranger in a tight-knot little town might have had a chore getting that close to an armed lawman, drunk or sober. How do *you* see it, Wagner?"

"Am I in charge here, like you said?"

"You sure are. She's in a position to complicate me."

Wagner nodded grimly. "I'm sorry, Miss Nancy, but since I never laid you, it's my duty to arrest you for the murder of the late Sheriff MacTavish by means of a lethal she-male weapon and likely a knife, too."

Then, as the blonde wailed like a banshee, Wagner turned to Longarm and said, "One of us oughta go get some help putting them on ice and her in the lockup, right?"

Longarm nodded. "She could use a doc, too. You stay here and I'll go deputize you some help. Then I'm going on out to Scots Wells to straighten the rest of the mess out. We'll do the paperwork when I get back, and I've got deputies to see her to the Denver Federal Court. I reckon two grown lawmen can handle her, now that she's wounded."

Wagner agreed and Longarm went out to mount Petunia and ride. As he passed the schoolyard, Tillie Baldwin ran out—fully dressed, of course—and called out that she'd heard the gunshots.

He reined in and nodded down at her. "That was me and some murderers, ma'am. Guess who won?"

"I'm so glad. Have you time to . . . ah . . . read with me some more?"

"Not just now, thanks. But I surely mean to before I head back to Denver. It's likely to take Lord knows how long to straighten all the details out hereabouts. So we'll manage something. I suspicion we missed a few pages."

He heeled Petunia into a lope and rode on, grinning. He wondered if old Fiona would forgive him, now that everything was going to turn out all right for all the infernal clans. He wondered why it mattered, given her delicate condition. There were lots of pretty gals in Scots Wells, and he suspected he was going to be their hero for the next few days.

But a promise was a promise, and he meant to spend at least one night with good old Tillie on the way back.

If his strength held out.

Watch for

**LONGARM
IN VIRGINIA CITY**

sixty-second novel in the bold
LONGARM series from Jove

coming in January!

Longarm fans gather round—

LONGARM

AND THE LONE STAR LEGEND

The Wild West will never be the same! The first giant Longarm saga is here and you won't want to miss it. LONGARM AND THE LONE STAR LEGEND features rip-snortin' action with Marshal Long, and introduces a sensational new heroine for a new kind of Western adventure that's just rarin' to please. Jessie Starbuck's her name and satisfaction's her game... and any man who stands in her way had better watch out!

So pull on your boots and saddle up for the biggest, boldest frontier adventure this side of the Pecos. Order today!

—— 515-07386-1/$2.95